"I'll give you money on one condition."

Rudi's offer stunned Arabella. It had all been too easy. The word "condition" made her suddenly hesitant. "But I couldn't possibly allow you to."

"Why couldn't you allow it?" Rudi asked cynically.

"Because," she stammered, "why should you? You hardly know my father."

"I wouldn't be doing it for him. I would be doing it for you, Arabella." Rudi's voice was almost tender.

"For...me?" For a second she could hardly believe what he'd said. A wave of pure joy raced through her.

"Yes." Rudi's voice was matter-of-fact, giving no sign of sharing her feelings. "And only, Arabella," he added, "if you agree to become my wife."

Rudi had spoken the words Arabella had dreamed of for so many years, but with one exception—the word love....

Alexandra Scott was born in a small Scottish village. She married an English soldier, and their travels, which took them to the Far East and various parts of Europe, proved to be good preparation for her later career as a writer. She had always wanted to write a book but was reluctant to actually try until she and her husband eventually settled in Yorkshire and he signed her up for a writers' course. She still has that wonderful, exciting feeling each time one of her books is accepted.

Books by Alexandra Scott

HARLEQUIN ROMANCE
2506—LOVE ME AGAIN
2514—THIS SIDE OF HEAVEN
2554—CATCH A STAR
2585—LOVE COMES STEALING
2604—BORROWED GIRL
2663—STORM WARNING
2769—WILDFIRE

Don't miss any of our special offers. Write to us at the following address for information on our newest releases.

Harlequin Reader Service
901 Fuhrmann Blvd., P.O. Box 1397, Buffalo, NY 14240
Canadian address: P.O. Box 603,
Fort Erie, Ont. L2A 5X3

An Old Affair

Alexandra Scott

Harlequin Books

TORONTO • NEW YORK • LONDON
AMSTERDAM • PARIS • SYDNEY • HAMBURG
STOCKHOLM • ATHENS • TOKYO • MILAN

Original hardcover edition published in 1987
by Mills & Boon Limited

ISBN 0-373-02868-7

Harlequin Romance first edition October 1987

CHAPTER ONE

'DAMN KULU,' she thought, the smile painted on her face as she bent her head to hear what the Minister was saying, his heavily accented English requiring some concentration. Besides, he was gazing at her as if he had never seen a woman before. Arabella encountered a chilly glance from his wife, extracted herself with a smile and moved on.

'Damn Kulu.' The mild imprecation came into her head again as she joined another chattering group in the large reception room, elegant, perfect yet curiously sterile as such apartments so often are, not really for living in. Why, she wondered, should she be expected to endure such boring evenings merely to publicise the new designs her employer was promoting this season, and largely because he was feeling resentful about the inroads being made into the UK market by German fashions? She was just his model, not his PR girl, although, being Kulu, he was scarcely likely ever to require such a thing.

A cold trickle ran all the way down her back and she shivered, cursing her brilliant employer again. Why on earth had she allowed him to dictate what she should wear? This particular dress, slit down the length of her spine, nape to waist, was enticing enough, but it looked like one sure way of catching a chill, although she would hardly have suspected Frau Steffan's ultra-modern house on the fringes of Berlin's Grünewald to have been subject to draughts.

Again she felt the spooky sensation run through her, a goose-walking-over-the-grave feeling, and cast a swift glance behind her in the direction of the door. And then her heart stood quite still; for an eternity she stopped breathing; everything, all the chattering commotion about her, was blotted out. The world slowed, halted on its axis as their eyes met, held.

Then her heart was racing, breath was hurrying from her lips, the blood that had drained away was flooding back to her cheeks, the roaring that had been so loud in her ears fading into the normal incomprehensible gabble and clatter of the typical cocktail party. She blinked, half convinced he would have disappeared, but he was still there, still staring, that intense, faintly narrowed look so typical of how he had once been, although almost everything else about him had changed.

He was older. That obvious fact was so unpalatable that she felt a painful blow to her chest before recognising that the passing years—five, nearly six—had done nothing to diminish him as a man. The opposite, in fact, for whereas the Rudi Schlegel she had known had always had masses of natural style and distinction, now he had the means, the money then so totally despised, to indulge his flair.

Or perhaps—she flicked a glance at the woman standing so close to him, so far totally unaware that she had lost her companion's attention, the proprietorial hand on his sleeve notwithstanding— perhaps after all he had decided to trim his principles and marry for money. It was possible: she looked a very formidable, single-minded lady, and she might have the force of character to succeed where Arabella had so signally failed in the past.

'If you imagine for a moment that I'm going to be a kept man, some kind of gigolo then you're much more stupid than I thought you were!' He had hissed the words at her in a whisper, full of the stiff-necked pride of the young and poor which she had been too inexperienced then to recognise. Then she had seen only that her father's wealth and generosity were

being thrown back at her. If only they had known . . .
On both sides the gestures were futile, the foolish
juvenile generosity as much as the pride which
rejected it.

And now there he was, standing like something out
of a twenties movie, some kind of reincarnation from
Brideshead Revisited, surveying her through those
deep-set unsmiling eyes, and she knew with absolute
certainty that her own thoughts were finding echoes
in his brain. He reached into a pocket and withdrew
a gold case, from which he extracted a cigarette and
lit it. His eyes above the short bright flame held hers
with such total possessiveness that she couldn't free
herself. Every detail was being imprinted on her
mind.

His suit was charcoal-grey flannel, impeccably
tailored with a faint white line emphasising the tall,
powerful shape, lean and taut now at . . . what was
he? she asked herself, pretending she had to think
about it. He must be thirty-one, for he was eight
years her senior . . . at thirty-one as he had been at
twenty-six.

His shirt was dark blue with a white collar,
tie broad-striped in black, blue and maroon. A
handkerchief in a pale shade of grey showed at his
breast pocket, and almost inconsequentially she
noticed the flower he was wearing in his buttonhole.
A cornflower. And suddenly she was remembering
what she had almost forgotten, she who had thought
it impossible to obliterate the slightest detail no
matter how she tried, remembering his inclination, if
they were walking along a road, to pluck a flower
from the wayside. It didn't matter if it were a piece
of heather filched from someone's rockery or a forget-
me-not from a verge; he would tuck it into his
buttonhole, or more often into the neck of his shirt,
always finding a matching one to place gypsy-fashion
behind her ear.

Today his hair was different. Gone the relaxed

longer hair so fashionable then; now it was cut fairly
short, parted on the right and slicked back severely.
It was thick and dark as ever, but its present style
symbolised more than anything just how the years
had passed, how much he had changed. And yet . . .
Such an admission was painful, for she had never
imagined she would find a man more potent and
attractive than the image she had carried in her heart
all these years. And yet that was exactly what he had
become. Harder and more ruthless, she suspected,
but much more—overwhelming; even at this distance
he could effect the most powerful reaction deep down
in her stomach.

'Darling!' It was Kulu's sudden appearance at her
side which brought her right back from the past to
the here and now, her mind swinging away from what
might have been. Without fully understanding what
was happening she allowed her employer's hand on
her elbow to impel her to the far end of the room. 'I
have someone longing to meet you.' His voice was
full of the liquid tones and resonances of his native
Greek, exaggerated for the present occasion. He was
too much the complete showman to miss such an
opportunity. 'Be good, Bella,' he whispered warningly
while continuing to smile devastatingly, 'she's as ugly
an an old crow, but I want her to believe that in my
creations she can look like you.'

'I'm tired.' Her cry was of panic more than
complaint. 'I want to go home.'

'After this, I promise.' Then loudly, 'And this,
Gräfin, is my top model, Arabella Smythe. Bella,
darling, the Gräfin of Schwandorf.'

She wasn't as ugly as an old crow. While Arabella
went through all the correct motions she was
registering that fact. Her mind, trying to cope with
the stunning shock she had just suffered, was now in
desperate search of diversion. No, the Gräfin was just
a woman approaching middle age, beginning to realise
her looks were fading. It was only Kulu, with his

absolute standards of female beauty and his streak of cruelty, who would have described her so unkindly. Often she had wondered how he would react to his own ageing process. Now he was at the height of his powers and fame, but neither would last indefinitely.

But no matter how she concentrated her mind on someone else's problems, Arabella could not quite wipe away the certainty that somewhere behind her, out of sight of even the huge elaborate mirror on the wall ahead, her own past lay in wait and ready to strike.

So when Kulu came to her rescue again she turned to him in relief, her pleading expression designed to remind him of his earlier promise.

'You will excuse us, *Gräfin*.' He swept her with dark slumbrous eyes. 'Arabella requires her beauty sleep, you know. I hope we shall meet again, *gnädige Frau*.' And with a slight bow he turned away, guiding his charge masterfully towards the door.

'Brilliant, darling.' For an instant he leaned his cheek against hers, dropping a brief caress on her skin. 'She'll be round to see us before the week is out. I could see her absolutely devouring the dress you're wearing. Now,' he straightened up, 'where is Frau Steffan? We must say goodnight to her before we go. Oh, and Bella, you *will* remember to thank her for letting you have the run of her stables while we are in Berlin. Ah,' his voice grew louder, more expansive as their hostess materialised in front of them. And Arabella, who had been praying that she would escape without a personal encounter, found herself hypnotised by the tall figure who dwarfed the small stout outline of Frau Steffan. In a dream she heard her employer embarking on an extravagant speech while she and Rudi looked at each other. So immersed was she in a tumult of feeling that she jumped when his name was spoken—the same . . . almost, as the one that she had known.

'And Rudi von Schlegel,' Frau Steffan gushed. 'Of course you have heard of him. Our latest celebrity.'

'Indeed, Frau Steffan.' Kulu spoke loftily. Beside himself, all other celebrities paled into insignificance, but his commercial sense compelled the introduction of his number-one girl. 'You have met Arabella Smythe, Frau Steffan, but perhaps Herr von Schlegel . . .'

'Oh, but yes.' His voice . . . How could she have forgotten how its depth and power had always managed to excite her physically, to make her flutter and tremble? 'Arabella and I have met.' The sombreness of his face implied a recollection which offered little to be excited about. 'Many years ago. And in Berlin, as it happens.' His eyes skimmed her face and shoulders. 'How are you, Arabella?'

Arabella. And in that cold formal tone. When once it would have been, *Liebling, Liebchen*, or most tenderly of all, *mein Schätzchen*. She could recall shivering in his arms while that dark, persuasive voice had murmured all the endearments he could think of. But now . . . Her face was as stiff as her smile was brilliant.

'I'm well, Rudi. And you?' Blessing the sophistication the years had brought, she raised an eyebrow in what she hoped was a friendly, detached way.

'Yes.' He nodded briefly, at the same time allowing his glance to rest for a moment on the man whose hand lay on her bare arm. Arabella felt the tension in Kulu's long fingers; he was the last man to welcome competition, and even Rudi's obvious prosperity could not keep the sulky note from his voice.

'Come then, Bella; it's time we got home to bed.'

Arabella had no idea whether he chose his words deliberately, but they brought a swift rush of warmth to her cheeks which she knew would not escape the close attention of the other man. But before they could move away towards the hall they were interrupted by a torrent of German, and the woman whom she had seen earlier, the one who she had imagined might be Rudi's wife, blocked her path. Certainly she was attractive enough, although she would not have thought that blonde, well-built Rhine-maiden style would have appealed to him.

But it appeared she was not Frau Schlegel, or Frau *von* Schlegel, she corrected herself sarcastically for she was being introduced as Fräulein Klara Steyr, and Kulu was bowing over her hand with all the gallantry he could muster, was murmuring something about music and the opera, which naturally forced Arabella to remember the name.

Klara Steyr, of course, was one of the most famous German singers of the day, and even now was performing in her home town, so what more natural than that Rudi would be found in her company? With his love of music—one of his jobs when they had met was as opera critic on an important Hamburg daily— it would be hard to imagine anything more likely.

But when she flicked a glance in his direction, Arabella saw that his attention was all on Kulu, appraising that performance, a hard little smile curving his lips. Then suddenly, unexpectedly, he was watching them no longer; his eyes held Arabella's, probing, intense, determined. And her veneer of sophistication crumbled, eyes widened in shock and dismay, her heart began its agitated tattoo and her breast rose and fell rapidly in a blatant display of her feelings.

'Kulu.' Impulsively she laid her fingers on his sleeve.

'Yes, darling.' In public he always responded to a gesture from a beautiful woman, and was instantly all attention, which only Arabella knew was insincere. 'We're going now.' And a few minutes later they had left the palatial house and were driving back towards the city and the flat just off Theodore Heuss Platz, shared, despite the impression he had tried to give, with three other models.

Arabella huddled, cold and shivery, in a corner of

the car, silently trying to come to terms with what had happened, making no response to Kulu's excited conversation, which consisted largely of self-congratulation and anticipation of the furore his new collection would cause when it was unveiled within the next few days. But at last he became aware of her withdrawal, and looked at her curiously.

'What's the matter, Bella? You can't be as tired as all that.'

'Can't I?' She shrugged. 'Unlike you, Kulu, I don't find much stimulation in trying to flog beautiful clothes to women who have more money than sense.'

'Come on, darling. It's your bread and butter as much as mine. Don't tell me you have scruples.'

'No, not really. Only sometimes the whole scene begins to seem so tedious. After all, Marks and Spencer produce decent clothes at a fraction of the price.'

'Even they have to have their clothes designed.'

'Yes, I know.' She sighed heavily as an indication that she was prepared to leave the argument there.

'Must be a touch of *Weltschmertz*.' Kulu swung the car off the road on to the decline that led to the underground garages connected with their apartment. 'This is the place to get it, they say. All those decades of sorrowful history. I wonder,' by now they were swishing upwards in the smooth lift, 'that man we met, Bella.' He was frowning in concentration. '*What* did Frau Steffan say his name was?'

'Rudi Schlegel. Von Schlegel,' she made the instant correction.

'That rings a bell with me. Something to do with writing or . . .'

'Writing?' Now he had all her attention. For hadn't Rudi dreamed of writing a great novel all those years ago when he had been merely a hack journalist—his description, others appeared to value his talents much more highly—a hack journalist for several Berlin and West German newspapers?

'No, maybe I'm wrong.' Reaching their floor they walked along the carpeted corridor and Kulu put his key into the lock. 'I just can't remember for the moment, Bella. I'll have to make enquiries tomorrow . . . Well,' he pushed the door closed with one foot, 'you can go to bed, darling, if you feel so tired. It's quiet as the grave now, so I suppose the others are snoring their heads off. Thank God!' He yawned and stretched. 'I'm pretty tired, too, so I'll see you in the morning.'

And Arabella was only too glad to escape, to begin to sort out her disordered emotions as fragmented memories began to scatter around her. Like shards of glass, and just as comfortable.

Almost six years since she had met him in Hamburg and had followed him to Berlin. It had been an idyllic summer, throbbing hot; she had just left school and had come across to brush up her German before going on to university. That had been the theory, but most people she had met had seemed more intent on practising their English than sharing the secrets of their own complex language with foreigners.

But she had had the most wonderful carefree time after she had broken into the groups of students who were just at the most questioning stage of their existence. It seemed that protesting students from all over Europe and America had congregated that year to plot revolution with the arrogance of youth and with no intention of putting any of their plans into action. In that first week she learned more about anarchy than she could have imagined, found it all highly stimulating once she came to terms with the fact that it was just talk.

Ridiculously, it was in Willi's *Bierhalle*—how often in the subsequent weeks they had laughed at the unromantic setting—that she had first seen Rudi Schlegel. She had been taken there by Ernst and was smiling at something he had said when she looked up and found herself the subject of Rudi's scrutiny. The way in which his eyes held hers, with warm possessive intimacy, made her smile fade and become a shadowy suggestion about her mouth, and she lost track of what was going on about her. As had happened tonight, in fact.

Arabella shivered, slumped down on to the stool in front of the dressing-table, and began aimlessly to reach for a pot of cream. Would he think she had changed? The wide eyes tried to recall what she had once been. Dark hair, long and thick, less unruly now than then. Now it was expertly cut and shaped, gentle waves framing her face in skeins of brown silk, ends flicking upwards, pretending to be casual.

Then he had thought her beautiful. In that, he hadn't been the first and certainly was not the last, but his assertion was retained long after all others were forgotten. Almost every word he had spoken to her she remembered, and those were among the first. The very first were when he managed to insert himself between her and Ernst.

'Tell me who you are,' he commanded with a touch of arrogance but as if much depended on her answer.

'Arabella Smythe.' She had been too young to deal in sophisticated procrastination. Already her eyes were adoring. What girl could fail to be overwhelmed at being singled out by this man? She sensed envious glances from the other girls about the table, a determination to attract him away from the English girl.

'Arabella Smythe.' Spoken by him in that slight accent with an attractive rolling of consonants, the name seemed to imbue her with a new and mysterious personality. 'I am Schlegel.' That, apparently, he considered explanation enough, but already he had been introduced as Rudi.

'You . . . you work in Hamburg?' She had been painfully shy and gauche, quite unlike herself, for even then she was neither of those things.

'No.' He smoked thin black cigars and lit one then,

pushing the smoke away with a hurried, impatient breath. 'I am a Berliner. Soon, I must return there. I wonder, Arabella Smythe, if I could persuade you to come there with me.' And, crazily, that was what she did.

Later, he had walked back with her to the house where she was staying with Ernst's family, pausing on the way to pluck buttercups which had seeded themselves on the path. One was for his buttonhole; another he had held under her chin, had asked if she liked butter, had kissed her.

It was almost the first time she had been kissed, and certainly the first time it had meant anything to her. Over the years she had lost count of the times she had tried, struggled almost, to recapture some of the magic. But in other men's arms it was impossible to attain, that bewildering, exciting weakness and joy. Even thinking of it filled her with such longing that she wanted to blot out the intervening years, to get back to what might have been and . . . Oh, who was she kidding?

Impatiently she slapped cream on to her face and pulled at her earrings so hastily that tears added to the brilliance of her eyes. Who are you kidding? she demanded sorrowfully of her reflection. There was no might have been; quite simply it had been the most beautiful and fulfilling time of her life. For a few short weeks she had been intoxicated with the joy of life and love, blessedly protected from the future which was to hold more than one person's share of anguish and unhappiness.

And that was why she must continue to wipe it from her mind, why she must refuse to go over it again right now, no matter how great the inclination. She just wasn't in the mood to cope with reopened wounds, and yes, she would—with great determination she pulled at the light switch and slipped between the sheets—she *would* go to sleep.

'Off you go, then, Bella.' Kulu observed her over the top of his heavily rimmed spectacles, tossing aside the letter he had been reading and passing his coffee cup over for a refill. 'But don't do anything foolish. Horse-riding in the Grünewald is all very well, but that is not why you came to Berlin. Try to remember you're here to show the collection, not to break your neck *before* the *Hausfraus* have the chance to appreciate my genius.'

'I'll try not to break my neck till afterwards,' Arabella replied drily, but she paused to smile and shake her head at him. He was the most unreasonable man she had ever met, almost a tyrant, but in spite of everything she was fond of him. 'But if I do let you down, I'm sure Caroline will be able to stand in for me.'

'Nonsense.' Kulu accepted the coffee from Caroline Noble who was sitting opposite him at the kitchen table. 'The dresses are designed with a special girl in mind—you know that, Bella. Caroline couldn't possibly carry off the cream chiffon, just as,' he ignored the younger girl's little murmur of protest, 'you, Bella, would look dreadful in her black lace.'

Arabella and Caroline rolled eyes at each other, and as Arabella made for the door of the flat, Kulu's voice, protesting that it was time the other two girls, still asleep in the largest bedroom, were awake and dressed, followed her into the hall.

On the taxi journey to the house which they had visited the previous evening, Arabella felt her lips curve affectionately as she thought of her employer. His bark was worse than his bite, and although he was so demanding, he was capable of kindness and consideration when you were least expecting it. With all he had on his mind right now, he had shown real consideration in asking if it would be possible for Arabella to borrow a horse once or twice while they were in Berlin. And she was so looking forward to the exercise, which would blow away all the gloomy introspection that threatened her sleep the previous night.

The taxi deposited her at the rear entrance as she had requested, and she found the stables without difficulty. It was a pity she hadn't thought to bring her old riding clothes with her, but she would be doing nothing more exacting than a steady trot, so her jeans and heavy shoes would be adequate. She had topped her checked blouse with a V-necked pullover in yellow, and her hair was caught back in a ponytail, knotted with a silk scarf.

In no time at all she was riding gently along one of the hundreds of paths which led through the woods, trying, as she had been trying since she woke that morning, to keep her mind away from the strangeness of her meeting with Rudi Schlegel. But at last, giving in to the impossibility, she allowed herself the indulgence of going through every second of what had happened at the reception.

A writer. Much of the bitterness and pain had gone, she was able to reflect in a detached way now that she had recovered from the shock of their meeting. A bestselling writer. Well . . . it had always been on the cards, and she ought not to have been surprised. Even then, he had had that air about him, the air of a man who knew where he wanted to go and who would reach his goal. And that was probably the source of his present affluence—not his operatic companion, as she had at first decided.

A shaft of totally unexpected jealousy coursed through her veins at the recollection of that woman's hand on his sleeve. She drew a shuddering breath, her heels jabbed into the plump sides of her mount, surprising the placid mare into a burst of speed that could have passed for a trot.

It was beautiful in the woods on a morning like this. Her sigh was sheer enjoyment with just a seasoning of nostalgia. How many times had she remembered the Grünewald with the sun filtering through a canopy of soft green, the sand-coloured earth chequered in a changing pattern of light and shade? It was blissful to move through the trees at this sedate pace, the hoofs making a comforting thudding sound on the thick carpet of composted foliage.

Uncertain when she first became aware of the louder clump of hoofs behind, Arabella pulled on the reins, encouraging the mare towards the side of the path to enable the other rider to pass easily. But when the outline of the huge black stallion came within her line of vision, her head jerked as some kind of premonition jangled a warning and she looked up into the impassive features of Rudi Schlegel. Instinctively she pulled her mount to a halt, watching while his pranced forward for a few paces then turned and came back towards her.

'Arabella.' She had forgotten how his voice could sound when it would linger, low and throbbing, over her name. In spite of all her intentions she felt warmth in her cheeks and body; if she had allowed it, she would have been overwhelmed with pleasure. But of course that was exactly what she would not permit, so after what was surely an eternity she was able to smile coolly and speak his name in a more or less normal voice.

'Rudi.' Her gloved hand moved to subdue an unruly strand of hair and his eyes followed that gesture. 'I didn't expect to see you.'

'No?' Polite scepticism was in the raised eyebrow. 'But I ride here every morning.'

'I didn't know.' Her smile was brief, and at the same time a touch on the reins made the mare give up her gentle cropping at a tuft of grass and move slowly forward. Without glancing again in his direction, she knew that he was following. Any other course would have been impossible.

And of course he was there, just at her elbow. Had she turned and reached out she could have touched him, but naturally she didn't, had no inclination to do so in spite of hammering pulses. In fact, the longer they rode on in silence, the less she was able to control the surge of panic . . . If only he would speak, just say something. A sob gathered in her throat, but before it found expression they emerged quite suddenly into a clearing at the far side of which was a typical *Gasthaus*—she had always thought them straight out of the Brothers Grimm—bathed in golden sunlight. Through a gap in the trees she saw a swathe of soft green turf leading down to an inlet of the Havel. The water danced with sparkling brilliance reminding her of another time. Oh, damn . . . But at least the clearing itself was not one she remembered; for that she was grateful . . .

'You would like some *Kaffee*, Arabella?' As he spoke he caught her reins, giving the impression that whatever her reply, her immediate course of action was already decided.

'Well . . .' She looked at the dark gloved hand in preference to the face which she knew was so intent on hers. 'Well, yes. Thank you.'

She slid from the saddle before he had the chance to help her, stood watching while he tethered both animals to a low-hanging branch where they could forage a little. And all the time she was wishing, with emotional excited anguish, that their paths had not chanced to cross this morning. She wasn't ready for it. Not yet. Not yet.

But still . . . She had noticed in that first shocked glance how much more he resembled the man she had once known. Dressed as he was this morning in tight cord breeches and polo-necked sweater, hair tumbled by exertion, he seemed to have shed several years. He was more like the man she loved than the bestselling writer could ever be. Had loved. She made the mental correction with a tiny frisson of impatience. *Had* loved, for of course she had got over her affair with him years ago. But now, with that easy, relaxed, more familiar air about him, it was easy to . . .

'Shall we go?' She had no idea how long he had been standing waiting, doubtless watching the play of emotions across her face, but she turned instantly, trying to be unaware of his fingers on her elbow. Even the thickness of a wool pullover and cotton shirt didn't offer complete insulation.

She sat at one of the tables on the veranda, heard him give his order to a woman who was hovering in the doorway. While she pulled off her gloves she tried to look relaxed, but that was less easy when he came to sit opposite, for then she was forced to look across the table at him. So close! Agitation rose in her like a storm, her fingers clenched as she fought for control.

'Well, Arabella.' If he was remembering the past then he was concealing it more successfully. From his pocket he took a slim gold case, offered it to her, watched her shake her head, asked her permission, then took out a cigarette and lit it slowly, lazily. 'So . . .' the intense eyes narrowed against the plume of smoke, '. . . you are back in Berlin.'

Ignoring a thread of hysteria which told her to deny it, she heard her voice, calm and detached, agree with him. If he was unmoved by their situation then she would be too, and her smile verged on the sincere. 'I was *so* pleased when Kulu decided to bring his collection out here.'

'Kulu?' His frown suggested the name displeased him. 'He is your employer?'

Arabella shrugged. 'Among other things.' She could not have explained why she chose to compound the impression Kulu had sought to give last night. Self-protection, she might have said if pressed. And there was an element of truth in her words. Kulu was also a friend, who helped her with her income tax, and dished out advice on all kinds of things. Not that his advice was often worth following, but . . . For at least ten seconds Rudi had been studying the glowing tip of his cigarette, but suddenly he looked up and straight into her eyes. So sudden, so percipient was his look that she felt wholly disorientated.

'I am surprised to find you in such a job, Arabella.' At least his words were banal enough. 'What about the plans to go to university?' There was a hint of sarcasm before his smile deflected her silent cry of misery. 'Or maybe I'm wrong, and you did fulfil your dearest ambition as well as becoming a model.'

'No.' What did he know or care about her dearest ambition? The arrival of the coffee gave her time to regain her control. Then, as she put her cup to her lips, she saw his eyebrows raised in enquiry and she shrugged, determined that none of her pain would be on public exhibition. 'Why? Oh, the best-laid schemes, I suppose.'

She smiled, but there was a blankness about her as she looked beyond him to the swaying treetops, the wind sighing gently through their branches. Further still, a yacht skimmed across the blue surface, trailing white ribbons.

Now was not the time to reveal the anguish she had returned to England to face. Anguish piled upon anguish, the second almost certainly saving her from the first. Now was not the time, not when it was impossible to penetrate the dark impassivity of his face, but how she longed to know if he too was remembering, and perhaps regretting a little. She spoke with sudden determined lightness. 'And you?' Her life was not going to be scrutinised if she could help it. 'You seem to have achieved all you ever hoped for.' The little crash was her cup banging against her saucer; she linked her fingers together, supporting her chin. 'Fame. Wealth. Tell me about the book.'

'Ah, the book.' There was a sardonic twist at the firm mouth. 'Perhaps it would be best for you to read it.' His glance was intense, penetrating. 'Then you can tell me what you think.'

She shrugged, falsely apologetic. 'Not if it's in German, I'm afraid. I've let that slip quite a bit.' She had, with deliberation, wiped it from her mind.

'Then perhaps in the English version. Already it's on the market here in Berlin, and it should reach the bookshelves in the rest of Europe in the next week.' Something in his manner gave her the idea that he was ready to leave the matter there.

But Arabella, hurt herself, was not above wanting to inflict some pain on him. Just a little, and guilelessly administered.

'And now you call yourself von Schlegel. I suppose vons are important in Germany.'

'Not really.' His dark eyes seemed to be telling her what a stupid young woman she was. 'I was born von Schlegel. But I decided to simplify things when I first came to Berlin to work. You remember those wild days when youth and protest were all?' He smiled grimly while rubbing out his cigarette in the large china ashtray adorned with bear and portcullis, advertising the light beer they had all drunk in the days he had just dismissed so lightly. She felt something squeeze at her heart and . . .

'Shall we go?' His enquiry was short and clipped; already he had risen to his feet as if anxious to end their encounter.

'Yes.' She had not quite finished, and raised her cup to her lips, more as a comment on his manners than because she enjoyed the dregs. The dregs. How appropriate. 'Of course.' She took her gloves from the table, slapped them against her faded jeans, lingering on the veranda while he settled the bill. Then, without speaking, they crossed to where the horses had been left.

He linked his hands for her, swinging her up into the saddle with an easy, powerful move, and stood there looking up at her for a few seconds before mounting himself and pulling his mount round.

'I must hurry.' It took her a few moments to recover from the penetrating power of that searing glance; her heart was still hammering uncomfortably against her ribs. 'This is a busy day and I promised not to be late.' She broke off abruptly when she realised he might not have heard, and a swift sideways glance showed a dark profile, apparently immersed in private thoughts. A moment later they had reached the drive leading towards the stables behind Frau Steffan's house. 'Well, goodbye, Rudi.' Her voice quavered dangerously until she regained control, 'It's been so nice meeting you again.' And with a jerk on the reins she had the mare trotting at a pace she had probably failed to achieve since her salad days.

They were turning into the gate before she looked back. But if she had been hoping to see Rudi Schlegel standing, still as a statue, looking after her, then she was disappointed; the paths were empty. Her meeting with him might have been a figment of her imagination.

If it had been as simple as that, then it might have been possible for her to dismiss him from her mind. As it was, no matter how she tried to concentrate on something else, he kept intruding; scenes from long ago slipped in and out of her mind like slides in a projector, blinding joy switching to utter despair in the course of a few exposures. Despair giving way, first to bewilderment, then to bitter anger when she understood at last that his desertion was total.

For years afterwards she had gone about with an ache in her chest, till quite suddenly she woke one morning to find it had gone. And she had been left with a sensation of emptiness, which was no improvement.

As she sat in the taxi on the way back to the flat, her smile twisted into a grimace as she recalled one of her early attempts to expunge Rudi from her memory. It had been two years after she had seen him, the pain was still raw, and she had made up her mind that the only way to get over one aborted affair was to embark on another. God knows she wasn't short of offers, and it was no big deal—an everyday event in the world where she now earned her living. Besides, she had liked Roy Lee; he had got her her first big commission, and he was less brash and pushy than some of the others. She could still remember the shock of meeting one man whose very first words were a suggestion they should go to bed together. 'I want to make love to you. Come and share my sack tonight,' had been his opening preamble, and he had been genuinely baffled when she turned away without replying. But Roy was kind, and wouldn't, like some of the others, be amused when she said it would be her first time; he would be tender and sympathetic.

So Arabella had packed her weekend case, but then at work on the Friday had got a call to say that her father had had a heart attack and she must go to the hospital right away. Afterwards, when her father was out of danger, it had occurred to her that Fate had chosen a drastic way of saving her from her own folly. Rather hard on her father, but on the whole she had no regrets.

It was an experience she had had no inclination to repeat, although inevitably there had been one or two men she liked quite a lot and with whom she desperately tried to fall in love. But sadly, none had come even close to wiping the memory of Rudi Schlegel from her heart.

For years she wondered what her reactions would be if they should chance to meet again, and she had long since made up her mind that, regardless of anything she might feel, cool detachment was what he would see. That conclusion had been easy enough when Rudi had become a distant shadowy image, but now that she had met him again she was having to struggle against the insidious attraction he had always held for her.

And his feelings for her? Over the years she had tormented herself seeking an answer to that. It was a torment to her *now*, for heaven's sake, because it was impossible to believe that any remnants of his old passion remained. Whatever else the years had done to Rudi Schlegel, they appeared to have cured him of his tender romantic streak.

Anyway, meeting him like this was maybe a blessing. She drew a deep, shuddering breath as she made up her mind very firmly on one point. A long time ago Rudi Schlegel had ruined her life, and there was no way that was going to happen a second time. Of *that* she was very sure.

CHAPTER TWO

As EVERYONE knew, work was the best possible cure for misery, and that was available in abundance during the next few days while the show was in preparation. At such times it was natural that the designer should suffer some degree of nervous tension, and Kulu was never one to do things by halves. So, by whatever natural law governs these things, everyone else had a ghastly time.

The girls—those whom he had brought with him and several who had flown out specially, the latter accommodated in a hotel—were all exhausted by the end of each day, with energy for little other than a sketchy meal, a shower and a blissful retreat to bed.

After several years Arabella was more or less used to the situation, but some of the younger models were brought to the edge of physical and nervous exhaustion.

'A..a..ah!' Caroline yawned loudly as she washed a pair of tights in the washbasin and squeezed them out. 'I'm shattered! Why does everyone think we lead glamorous lives? I've made up my mind to be a coalminer in my next existence.'

'What's that about coalminers?' Arabella stepped out of the shower, a fleecy towel wrapped about her, hair enclosed turbanwise by another. 'Did I hear you right, Caro?'

'Only that I wish I had been one instead of a model. I reckon it must be easier.'

'There are times when I might agree with you, though I doubt that you'd ever convince a miner! But

anyway, we'll have a break after tomorrow. Roll on
this time tomorrow night.' She sat on the edge of the
bath and began to rub her wet hair. 'I can't tell you
how glad I'll be to get on that plane out of Berlin.'

She couldn't have explained just why she said that,
and had no satisfactory reply for Caroline's surprised
query. 'Yes I *do* like the city,' she countered weakly,
'but like you, I'm exhausted and can hardly wait to
get home.' And I shan't feel safe till I do, she was
thinking when there was a sudden loud banging on
the door and Kulu was calling her name.

'It's a telephone call for you.' As he gave the
message he was hurrying through to the large
bedroom, now being used to store some of his most
precious secret creations. 'From London; your father,
I think.'

'Hello.' Although she had left the number with her
father she had not expected him to contact her; in
fact, he had been so immersed in some business
project that he had scarcely seemed to be aware that
she was to be out of the country for a time. 'Hello.
Dad?' It was a relief to recognise his voice. Since he
had had that heart attack after the crash she had
always been anxious, although just recently, when he
had seemed so much better, the worry had slipped
away to the back of her mind. But now, quite
suddenly, it was revived. 'Are you all right?'

'Fine, sweetheart. I'm fine.' But his voice and faint
laugh were not reassuring. 'How are things going?'

'Oh, everything is all right. Frantic, of course, but
that's just what you would expect at this stage. By
this time tomorrow night it'll all be over, and with
luck Kulu should have a huge order book.' Arabella
knew she was babbling on, but she felt an instinctive
reluctance to learn the real reason for her father's
call. 'Is Mrs Fisher looking after you all right? Seeing
to your meals and . . . everything?'

But the reassurance she sought was never offered,
for her father ignored the query. 'Look, Arabella, I

wanted you to know just in case you should read anything in the papers . . .'

'Dad, what is it?' She fought the rising tide of panic. 'Are you sure you're all right? Not ill or anything? If you are, I'll come home straight away.'

'No, I'm not ill.' Again he gave that slight bitter snort that suggested nothing less than amusement. 'I only wish it were that simple. And don't, whatever you do, give up your job; you'll need that in the months ahead.'

'*Dad* . . .'

'Okay, love, okay, I'll get on with it. I'm afraid I'm in a bit of a jam. The deal I was trying to negotiate has collapsed, and the result is that I've been left holding the baby. Anyway, it's a complicated story and I'm not going to bore you with all the ins and outs. The long and the short of it is that unless I can come up with a substantial sum of money within the next few days then I might become involved with the Fraud Squad and all the ramifications of that.'

'Oh, God . . .' Without realising she had spoken, Arabella groped behind for a chair to support legs suddenly turned to rubber.

'*Don't*, Arabella.' It wasn't exactly a sob in her father's voice, but near enough. 'Don't take it too hard, or that will finish me completely. It was for your sake I was trying to get back to where we once were. To give you all the things you were brought up to expect.'

'Oh, Dad,' her voice sounded thick, 'you should know none of that matters. We'd got over all that, and as long as your health was all right I didn't want anything else. The money didn't matter.'

'Yes, I've been a fool.' He sounded beaten, not the confident, breezy man who had gradually been restored after his huge property empire had disappeared in a monumental crash. 'I knew there were risks, but I thought I could bring it off. Only now I know I can't. I've lost my touch, and the people I was involved with . . . Well, the less said about them the better. Now I've told you, the worst is over; you can't imagine how I was dreading that . . . I think there might be some mention of it in tomorrow's papers, and I didn't want you to see it there.'

'But Dad,' her mind was racing wildly, searching for some kind of solution, 'there's the flat, surely you can raise some money on . . .'

'The flat, my love . . . is already gone. It was a loan on that that made it possible for me to get started again.'

'Oh Dad!' It was difficult to control the dismay that flooded through her, to eliminate the reproach from her voice. Their home, bought with what little had been saved from the crash, together with various bits and pieces of antique furniture left to Arabella by her mother, constituted their entire capital. About the latter she dared not enquire; later would be time enough for that, when she felt more able to cope.

'That's how it is, my love. Unless I can raise something close to a six-figure sum by next weekend then things are going to be pretty bad.'

'But there must be some way . . .' Prison. That was what he was suggesting, preparing her for, and that was something she couldn't bear for him. 'Someone must be able to lend you some money . . .'

'For money like that you need security, and that's exactly what I don't have.' Another grim little laugh. 'So unless you happen to have a philanthropic millionaire in mind . . .'

'I wish I had. Oh, I wish I had!' And the desperate wish echoed through Arabella's mind after she had replaced the receiver and run into her bedroom. She was chilled with standing in the hall for so long. Either that or she was suffering from shock. She rubbed frantically at almost dry hair, then pulled on some jeans and pullover.

Kulu. He would help. That was the only thought in her frightened mind, and she felt hope rise as she ran across, tapped at the door of his sanctum and went inside when he called.

'Bella.' His glance was cursory and frowning as his attention was distracted from the yellow silk ballgown he was studying. 'You spoke with your father?' His query was automatic, not really interested.

'Yes. Yes, I spoke to him, Kulu.'

'Good.' He stood back, head held critically to one side. 'I wonder . . .' A brief touch to the cascade of knots which fell from just beneath the bust. 'Bella?' Suddenly he frowned and looked up, dark brows pulled together in a way that would in normal circumstances have warned her to tread very carefully. 'You want something, I suppose; you know I can't work when distracted, and you are distracting me now. What *is* it?' he demanded edgily.

'Just,' her mouth quivered, her confidence in him abruptly shattered, so completely swept away that she couldn't understand why she was standing there, 'just that I've had some bad news.'

'Oh?' His frown deepened. 'Nothing, I hope, which will interfere with tomorrow's show.' There was even a hint of menace in the way he looked at her. 'You know I consider you my best girl, Bella, and I couldn't possibly manage without you.'

'Oh, no.' Her smile turned into a grimace. 'No, Kulu, I'll be here, don't worry. It's just that my father's in a financial jam, and . . .' Impossible to admit that for just a few seconds she had hoped he might be able to help. '. . . and I wanted to confide in someone. But,' she turned to the door, 'I can see you're busy . . .'

'I'm never too busy to give advice.' Kulu came forward and prevented her from leaving by placing his hand on the closed door. 'It is serious, no?'

'I'm . . . I'm afraid so. He needs a large sum of money within a few days. I don't suppose, Kulu . . .' But even as she spoke she watched the guarded look come down over her employer's face, remembered how extremely cautious he was where money was concerned. 'I don't suppose you know anyone so filthy rich that a hundred thousand here or there won't matter.' This time her smile was a triumph, designed to conceal from him how close she had come to asking for financial help.

'Oh, I know plenty of them, *agapi mou*,' his expression relaxed a little, 'but unfortunately even the richest are inclined to be careful about the odd thousand, let alone a hundred thousand. A hundred thousand!' His eyebrows came together in disbelief. 'As much as that, Bella?'

'Almost.' She regretted the weakness which had allowed her to admit to a specific sum. 'But don't worry, Kulu; I'm sure Dad will know someone who can help out with a temporary loan. And that's all he needs really, just some cash to tide him over till things are settled.'

'Well, maybe he could borrow something on the house. You did tell me once that he owned the flat you live in.'

'Yes, of course. I'm sure that's what he'll do. It will certainly help, and . . .'

'Or,' Kulu interrupted with a sly sideways glance that she didn't see, 'there's always your friend from the other night.'

'My . . . friend?' Now he had her entire attention, though she was at first unable to understand how his mind was working. When she did, colour flooded her cheeks. 'Oh, you mean . . .'

'Yes, your writer friend, of course. I suspect he must have some spare cash floating about looking for an investment . . .'

'Oh, I couldn't possibly.' With an effort she regained control and her manner was throwaway. 'I don't know him all that well. Besides, it's not what you would call an investment, is it? Not really.'

'You know'—Kulu reached into the pocket of his shirt and pulled out a packet of mints, offered one to

Arabella, and when she shook her head, took one himself, surveying her through perceptive eyes—'you intrigue me, Bella. You always have. How old are you? Twenty-three, is it not, and yet . . .'

'And yet what?' She was immediately, betrayingly defensive.

'And yet,' he continued with the shadow of a smile which told her he had drawn some conclusions from her reaction, 'of all my girls, you are the only one I've never seen go overboard for one man or another. Oh,' he held up a hand as if she had been about to protest, 'I know you're never short of men friends, but I've never seen you react strongly to any one of them.' He paused before delivering his sting. 'Not till the other night.'

'The other night.' She forced a little frozen laugh. 'Do you mean at Frau Steffan's, Kulu? You're letting your imagination run out of control . . .'

'I think not,' he said softly. 'Do you know, Bella, I saw him watching you for a full five minutes before you turned round. At first I thought it just the normal male reaction to a more than pretty girl, but then I realised that you were subconsciously aware of his eyes on you; you were uneasy without understanding why. And then at last you turned round, and the expression on your face . . . Well, it told such a lot.'

'Really.' Arabella felt her fingers biting into her palms and made a determined effort to relax. 'Tell me then, Kulu, just what my expression revealed. Then I'll say whether or not you're right.'

'Well,' he shrugged with mock modesty, 'you know I studied psychology before taking up art . . .'

She nodded briefly. Like all those who came into contact with Kulu, she had heard of his years in the Department of Psychology at Athens University, and like most she felt a fair amount of scepticism. There was a much more believable tale circulating that he had worked from the age of twelve in his father's tailoring shop in a tiny back street off the Plaka before venturing out on his own, and that his success was as much due to sheer exhibitionism as to talent.

'. . . So,' he continued after a few moments' consideration, 'I would say that you and Herr von Schlegel had at one time a more than platonic relationship.'

'If you're saying, Kulu, that at one time, light years ago'—it caused physical pain to desribe what had been so intense and precious in such careless terms— 'Rudi and I had a mild, casual flirtation, then I confess. Your years at university were not entirely wasted.' The little dig was impossible to resist.

'A casual flirtation, you say? I thought that sort of thing went out with the crinoline.' He raised a sceptical eyebrow. 'He does not give the impression of a man who is casual about everything. But if you tell me it is so then I must believe you.' His tone denied the assertion. 'Tell me what happened.'

Arabella shrugged. 'Nothing *happened*. I was just over here for a few weeks on holiday and then I went home. Rudi, I think, returned to the East Zone. That is where his family lived. And I'd never seen him again till the other night.'

'Ah?' He continued to survey her critically. 'Well, I should say *he* could be the one to help you in your present difficulties. Think about it, Bella. And try not to worry. I don't want you looking like a hag tomorrow night.' And as if he had tired of the whole subject, he turned with a determined gesture to the dress he had been examining.

'I'll try, Kulu.' Like all the girls, she was used to his unflattering comments and accepted them with something approaching humility. 'And thank you . . . for letting me talk.'

'All right darling, all right.' He had forgotten her before she reached the door, and by the time she was in her bedroom she knew he would be totally absorbed in his collection. And on the whole, she decided, she didn't blame him. She only wished she

could do the same. But instead of having her mind
fixed on what was going to happen tomorrow, worry
about her father's situation lay like a weight on her
chest until, surprisingly soon, sleep blotted it out.

For the show Kulu had been fantastically lucky in
being offered, for a considerable fee, one of the most
elegant small palaces in the whole city. Built in the
eighteenth century, in the grandiose days of Frederick
the Great, it glittered with the rococo details which
were then so fashionable.

The grand staircase by which the models were to
descend to the hall was heavily gilded, while against
green marble walls hung mirrors ablaze with the lights
from crystal chandeliers. It was a glamorous if slightly
overwhelming setting, one which Kulu was finding
entrancing but difficult.

'You must,' he insisted at rehearsal as Caroline
walked along the raised catwalk, 'you *must* give it so
much *more*. Can't you *see*?' A dark hand raked
through his hair, eyes rolled heavenwards in despair.
'You are not coming downstairs in a Chiswick semi.
Here, possibly, came down the Empress of Germany.'
He pranced fancifully, hands on hips. 'Much more
drama. *You* are Empress of All the Russias. Please,
Caroline, or we might as well all go home.'

The day was so exhausting with practices and
fittings, constant rearrangements in the order of
presentation, discussions about various types of music,
rows with the sound engineer who did not speak
much English. In fact, it was only when Arabella
stepped in with a few words of translation that the
situation between the young man and Kulu calmed
down a little and the misunderstanding was smoothed
out.

'Well, he did want more *drama*!' Caroline whispered
to Arabella as they flew upstairs for yet another run
through.

'I don't think being cheeked by a mere workman

was exactly what he meant,' Arabella panted, and
hung on to the banister at the top, pausing for a
second to regain her breath, 'and especially in a
language he doesn't understand.'

'No, that's his line. He doesn't like seeing anyone
in the role he's made his own. Hey . . .' she threw
herself on to a stool and began to rummage among
the things on top of the dressing-table, '. . . has
anyone seen my lipstick? The *brown* one.' Her voice
rose to a wail. 'If I lose that then I shan't be able to
go on in that yellow dress. Evelyn!' She jumped up
and pounced on the girl who had just come into the
room, snatching something from her hand before the
other girl knew what was happening. '*Here* it is.' And
she began carefully to smear it over the full curve of
her lips.

'It isn't.' With an air of barely controlled desperation, Evelyn looked about her, appealing for support
from the roomful of girls who were all totally involved
in their own concerns. 'Arabella . . . Naomi . . . Has
anyone seen my lipstick?' But no one paid her the
least attention.

But as always seemed to happen, the utter chaos of
seven-fifteen was translated into a nearly impeccable
display on the dot of seven-thirty.

Arabella, an air of complete insouciance concealing
a wildly beating heart, wandered out of the room and
along the upper balcony among the elegant spectators
sitting in rows five deep on each side. Then, slowly,
one hand resting on the cool metal of the balustrade,
soothed by the muted sounds of Telemann, she
descended the impressive staircase. Gradually she felt
all the day's, and the previous evening's, tensions
melt away as she fell easily into the routine which
was so familiar. And which she loved.

Leaving the staircase, she advanced along the
catwalk, smiling faintly into the dazzle of lights which
dimmed the sea of faces turned in her direction.

'And here is Arabella.' Kulu's English could be so

attractive, so melting when he remembered to smooth out the faint Cockney accent he had acquired in his twenty years in London. 'Her cotton jersey dress in delicious pistachio looks good enough to eat. Notice the piping on the dropped shoulderline; the skirt is flowing and easy, as you can see.' Obediently Arabella did a whirl and felt the soft material swish about her legs before she began to move along the T-junction of the catwalk, hurrying out of sight as she heard Kulu begin to describe Naomi's dress.

Then, a wild dash up the back stairs, much narrower and less impressive than the front ones, clearly designed for the servants and very convenient on an evening such as this. She ran into the changing-room where a whole battery of hired seamstresses were waiting to help the models dress and make any tiny adjustments which might be necessary. After the green cotton, there was a cream-coloured linen, then a burnt orange sundress, dazzling, banded with black and utterly sophisticated. Her appearance in that drew the warmest burst of applause of the entire first half, increasing as she pulled off the face-hiding sunhat and shook out her hair. Then she swung her sunspecs by one arm while she strolled off, thankful that they had reached the interval.

Kulu descended on them with a torrent of suggestions and with not the faintest hint that he might be pleased with how they had performed. 'The lights are too bright. You're all cross-eyed when you come to the end of the walk. I've seen the lighting man and he's going to drop them just a bit, so for heaven's sake try not to frown. It quite spoils the effect.'

When they began again the concentration was mainly on casual afternoon dresses, pretty and immensely flattering in jewel shades but with just one or two of Kulu's ridiculous fun outfits to 'wake up the audience' as the designer put it, and to amuse as well, judging from the spontaneous laughter and applause which greeted their appearance.

For this Arabella was required to struggle into a pair of black leather shorts, tighter than her skin and with a matching bolero equally brief and revealing. With them she wore black tights scattered with red roses and a cartwheel hat with a cluster of roses on the brim.

'Just right for a wedding,' she murmured despairingly to Caroline as she caught her up on the return staircase. 'I only wish Kulu wouldn't inflict his ideas on us.'

But her next dress was her favourite of the entire collection, in a glowing shade of green shot with gold. The pure silk was as fine as gossamer, and each time she moved it caught the light, reflecting a subtle gleam from the chandeliers. Her reflection pleased her: her hair artistically dishevelled, cheeks glowing from her exertions as much as from the small amount of blusher she had applied before they began. Impulsively she touched her lashes with gilt, brushed a little more apricot on to her lips. Then she had to rush as she heard the notes that signalled her entrance.

At the back of her mind was a faint amusement as she listened to a description of her appearance. If by some mischance she had missed her cue, would Kulu have gone on regardless, expecting her to catch up if she could? In spite of everything the evening had been stimulating, had helped keep her mind from her main problem. She felt her smile slip as the weight of it threatened to swamp her again, then quickly adjusted it, stopping at the end of the catwalk to give the customary sway which took the material away from her body then brought it floating back again.

She smiled, eyes slightly narrowed, persuasive, sending encouraging messages to the spectators. And then . . . found herself looking directly into the impassive face of Rudi von Schlegel.

A stirring among the first few rows, a faint

uneasiness was all that brought her back to the
present, made her realise just how long she had been
standing there. A jerky little move took her round
and away only in time to avoid Evelyn who had
reached the foot of the stair. Her heart was thumping
madly as she reached the exit and blundered up the
stairs.

Rudi. And presumably he had been there all
evening, head to one side and listening to the woman
beside him. But who had he been with? She had
been so shattered that she hadn't even glanced at his
companion. But it was bound to have been a woman.
Men did not, as a rule, come to these occasions on
their own. Not unless they were in the business or
had some other interest.

And then, for some reason she could never
understand, Kulu's words of the previous evening
were hammering in her mind. 'Your writer friend—
he must have some spare cash floating about looking
for an investment . . .'

'Bella! For God's sake . . .' It was her employer in
the flesh, eyes flashing blackly with displeasure. 'What
on *earth* were you thinking of out there?'

'Out there?'

'I thought you had been turned to stone.'

'Oh, that.' She was able to sound casual. 'I felt a
bit giddy for a couple of seconds.'

'More like a couple of minutes. Well, I hope it
doesn't happen again, Bella. And *you*, Imogen . . .'

Arabella heard his voice going on while she allowed
herself to be extricated from the green dress, but her
mind was racing round. Was it possible that there
might be something in her employer's suggestion? If
by some chance Rudi had retained some feeling for
her, might that be put to her advantage? Or rather—
a tremor of fear trickled through her—to her father's
advantage. She was prepared to do anything to save
him. Anything.

The show ended with a bang. And although Arabella had not in the end been chosen to wear the wedding ensemble she was pleased rather than disappointed, for she was convinced that on this one outfit Kulu had gone wildly astray. A little fun was one thing, sending up a bride something else. Berliners, at least the older ones with money to spend on designer clothes, were notoriously conservative, and she didn't imagine that white knickerbockers with lace blouse and veil would go down all that well at the average sentimental city wedding.

Whereas her own dress, dreamy and romantic, would fulfil every woman's image of how she might look for a special meeting with a special man. Coming down the staircase, she was shrouded in a cape of velvet weighted round the hem so it fell straight and heavy to the floor. Modestly she bowed her head while she walked, drawing attention to her hair swept into a knot on the crown, showing a long slender neck.

Then, as she reached the foot of the stair, she unhooked the cape, tossing it over her arm as she moved forward, feeling the sensuous rustle of taffeta against her legs. The sound, the feel, the admiring sigh of pleasure from the audience, heightened her already racing pulses, and she struggled to avoid looking directly at the seat where she knew she would see him.

In the background she recognised a Strauss waltz, the seductive notes anything but calming, and without realising what she was about, her hand went protectively to her throat. And at that very instant her eyes sought his. For an extended moment she stood at the end of the walk, the warm colour of whipped cream enhancing the rich dark brown of her hair, emphasising the peachy texture of her skin, the wide eyes full of apparently unconscious appeal.

Slowly she turned, walking with unhurried grace, her heart still hammering wildly against her ribs, breathless with agitation caused by the dominating way his eyes held hers.

For a split second they had seemed to be divorced from all that was happening about them; everything else had faded. It was as if in some magical way the intervening years had been wiped away and they were back where they had been so long ago.

Wearily she climbed the staircase, trying to banish the uneasy feelings of guilt that assailed her. She had, having been tortured by indecision till the last moment, gone out to make a direct appeal, and the tension which had stretched between them assured her that Rudi had recognised her blatant message. And now, here she was, feeling somehow . . . degraded.

CHAPTER THREE

'ARABELLA.' Still she had not expected Rudi to come so quickly. The glass in her hand quivered, spilling some of the sparkling wine on to her skirt.

'Oh, hello.' With a tiny handkerchief she scrubbed at the spot on the black grosgrain, more to divert attention from her confusion than that the tiny mark was so noticeable. 'Sorry.' Relieved that her colour had died down a little, she smiled at him. 'You startled me.'

'Did I?' His tone doubted it, and his fingers were on her elbow, forcing her away from the group to which she had been attached. 'I wanted to talk with you, Arabella.' His voice was intense, and if she hadn't known otherwise she might have thought him nervous. Rudi Schlegel, nervous?

'Oh, really?' She raised her glass, surveying him with what she hoped passed for coolness over the rim, disturbed still more by the intensity of those narrowed eyes. She had the impression—no, not even that, a suspicion—that he was less in control of himself than he had appeared to be till now. The rise and fall of his chest under the elegance of dazzling cotton and dark suiting might have been a shade more rapid than usual; a nervous tongue passed over parted lips and . . .

But she was being foolish, allowing wishfulness to overcome reason, transferring her own closely guarded longings to him, when what she had truly been aware of was his apparent ability to see behind the protective façade she had erected.

'You must know it.' He spoke tensely, passionately almost, but still she felt he had little mellowness for her. 'When may I see you alone?'

'Oh?' She shrugged, with an effort wrenching her eyes from his, looking round, seeing nothing until the tall figure of her employer, the centre of a group of admiring women swam into her sight. 'I . . .' She couldn't think how to answer him.

'You mean,' his voice grew brittle, uncompromising, 'he may object to my seeing you?'

'Who?' Only when she raised her eyes again to his face did she realise that Rudi had followed her glance and put his own conclusion on what he saw. 'Oh, Kulu.' At once her senses were on the defensive. 'Why should he?'

'You are . . . living with him.'

'At the moment.' Her shrug spoke of a casual admission and somehow she missed the tightening of his jaw, the swift pulling together of his eyebrows might have been a warning. 'But he doesn't control everything I do.' Blandly she faced him.

'Then come and have supper with me.'

'All right.' Her plan was working more smoothly than she could have hoped. 'But what about Fräulein Steyr?'

'Klara did not arrive with me.' Dark eyes bored into hers.

'Oh?' She was weak and trembly, excited by the feelings his words caused. Relief. Pleasure that he had not brought the opera singer. 'Then . . .'

'Arabella.' It was Kulu at her arm, and she saw the disdainful way he regarded her companion before transferring his attention to his employee. 'The telephone for you.'

'For me?' The implication did not at first dawn on her.

'Yes.' He raised one of her hads to his lips while his other arm snaked round her waist, his cheek was pressed to the top of her head. 'From England, *agapi mou*. Come, I will show you . . .' And, ignoring Rudi completely, he led her away from the throng of people, through the huge hall where the catwalk was already being dismantled and into a small room at the back of the house.

Arabella sank on to the chair beside the desk, raising the telephone with shaking fingers and hardly noticing the door closing behind Kulu as he left her alone.

'Arabella!' Her father's voice was breathless and agitated. 'I've been trying to reach you all day.'

'Dad, we've just had the show. Has something happened?' Her voice trembled with worry and nervousness as she suspected the worst.

'Oh, I've managed to raise some money, love. Just about half of what I need, but . . . it's pretty desperate.' His voice faded, broke on a trembling gasp before he began again. 'And I just wondered if you have any ideas. If I could just lay my hands on another thirty thousand pounds I believe I could swing it . . .'

'But I can't think.' Arabella bit fiercely on one finger. 'Oh Dad, you must know . . . if only I *could* think of anyone who could help . . . I wonder, maybe I could raise a loan on the strength of what I earn and . . .'

'That would take time, love. Oh, I know I shouldn't be worrying you like this, but . . . I felt I just had to talk to someone . . . that's the worst part of it right now . . . no one to talk to. Anyway, I'll keep trying, and if you do come up with anything you will ring, won't you, Arabella?'

The conversation continued for another few minutes, but at last, when the ground had been retraced several times, Arabella said goodnight and replaced the receiver on the cradle. For a moment she sat, then, rising, walked over to the mantelpiece, watching her approach in the huge gilded mirror which hung on the wall above. A tall girl wearing an exquisite white blouse, lawn, heavily embroidered at the front and with wide billowy sleeves caught at the wrists.

A sob burst from her lips; she frowned, nibbled again at her fingers, then looked up in sudden alarm as the door opened and light came flooding into the dimly lit study. She was still trying to compose her features when Rudi closed the door, lying back against it for a moment, then coming forward, facing her in the glass.

'Arabella.' His voice throbbed disturbingly, forcing her to clench her fingers tightly, to control the wild urge she felt to throw herself against him in a frenzy of weeping. Oh, the comfort of being held close to his chest, his arms folded protectively about her.

But that, she thought with a stab of bitter amusement, would do his immaculate dark suit no good at all, to be messed up with a *mélange* of tears and creams and powders. Besides which she had no intention of allowing him to catch her at such a disadvantage.

'Arabella.' He spoke again, and at the same time his hand came out, turning her towards him, his face studying and doubtless noting all the evidence of worry and distress.

'Yes.' It was hard to divorce her emotions from the powerful touch of his fingers, burning through the material of her blouse, searing through to her skin.

'Something is wrong?'

'No, of course not.' She smiled painfully. 'Why should you think anything is wrong?'

'For God's sake!' He gave her a little shake. 'Do you think I can't *see*?' The flare of anger faded from his eyes as quickly as it had appeared. 'You had a telephone call here; that in itself suggests some urgency, and besides . . . All evening I have had the impression that you had something on you mind. You were less light-hearted than when we met the other day.'

'Nonsense. That was simply the worry of the

performance. We suffer from first-night nerves much the same as actors, you know. It's not such a different business.'

For a long moment after she had stopped speaking he just stood staring at her. She knew his eyes were absorbing every detail of her appearance. From the dark hair restored to her favourite casual style, waving gently over her forehead, flicking upwards at the ends, to the widely spaced eyes, the mouth that quivered nervously when he looked at it. She ran the tip of her tongue over dry lips.

'Shall we go?' The sudden suggestion surprised her.

'Go?' Warily she returned his look, worried that for a few unguarded moments she had revealed too much of her feelings.

The faintest of smiles curved the mouth, relaxing the harshness that characterised the new Rudi Schlegel. 'You did say you would have supper with me.'

'Oh, yes.' Her conversation was less than sparkling, she realised—certainly less than would be required to persuade a man like him to part with a considerable sum of money. 'I'll . . . just get my handbag.'

'Bella.' Caroline pounced as they were crossing the hall in the direction of the large reception room. 'I've been looking everywhere for you.' The look she slid towards Rudi was more than slightly interested. 'Kulu's going *mad*, and . . .'

'Where is he? I must just see him. Oh, this is Rudi Schlegel, Caroline.' She glanced at him. 'My friend, Caroline Noble. Excuse me for a moment; I can just catch him.'

When they were being driven through the brilliant-lit streets of West Berlin, Arabella huddled into one corner of the back seat, as far away from Rudi as she could manage, wondering with a flare of sheer panic just what she was getting herself into. If it hadn't been for her father's urgent need for money then nothing on earth would have induced her to be alone with him.

Quite simply, she had never got over that long-ago affair. The stab of jealousy she had experienced when she had come back to find him so obviously amused by Caroline confirmed that in the most definite way, had forced her to be honest with herself. She had even, wounded by the expression of relaxation on Rudi's face, been tempted to suggest waspishly that as they enjoyed so much each other's company, perhaps they ought to go out together, and that she would as soon return to the flat with Kulu. But at the last minute she remembered just what was at stake and had smiled at her friend, ignoring the look of disappointment when they had said goodnight.

'He did not mind?' Rudi's harsh enquiry from the opposite corner took her eyes from their study of the chauffeur's head, flickering in the direction of the dark outline of her companion.

'Who?' she pretended. Then, 'Oh, Kulu. Well, he wasn't delighted.' That was true; he had thought she ought to stay and try to persuade one or two undecided customers. 'But as I told you, I don't let . . . others'—the men I live with, her tone implied—'decide who I should go out with.' She paused. 'Where are we going?'

'To my house.' Even as she spoke the car turned between impressive stone gates, drew up in front of a large villa.

'Your house?' She allowed herself to be helped from the car while the chauffeur held open the door, and her eyes took in the spill of light from several windows, the quiet air of luxury suggested by everything she could see.

'*Ja*. Always I have promised myself a house on the edge of the Grünewald. Don't you remember?'

Yes, Arabella said silently, ignoring the sting of tears at her eyes. Only I thought you would have forgotten.

'No.' They reached the hall, her feet moved across deep-pile carpet the colour of fresh sage. 'No,' she smiled brilliantly over her shoulder, 'I had no idea.'

Supper was served by a middle-aged housekepper who disappeared after attending to the main course—delicious tender *Sauerbraten* served with horseradish, tiny carrots and french beans.

Arabella realised how hungry she was when she tasted the quails' eggs which formed the first course, and she ate the meat with considerable relish. I ought, of course, she reproved herself silently, to be pushing the food round my plate, too agitated to eat. Then she looked up, and the expression on Rudi's face drove the remains of her appetite away.

'Now tell me, Arabella.' They had finished coffee and Rudi stood leaning against the green marble mantelpiece, looking down at her while he lit a cigarette—there was a pang of sheer nostalgia when she saw him abstractedly flick the match alight with his thumbnail. He drew the smoke deep into his lungs, sucking in his cheeks, retaining it for a moment before exhaling. 'Tell me what is worrying you.'

Suddenly, and to her shame, she felt a tear slip down her cheek; the urge to release her burden was irresistible. But she tried to smile up at him.

'Oh, nothing.' She shook her head, feeling her hair dance about her face. 'At least, nothing that thirty thousand pounds wouldn't cure.'

The moment the words were uttered she was appalled. How could she have been so blatant about it all? It was almost like begging. And worse still—she wrenched her eyes from his, wondering if she was imagining that same wary look she had seen on Kulu's face in the same circumstances—wasn't she practically offering herself to him? Shame burned in her cheeks.

'Thirty thousand pounds?' His voice was even enough, and she risked a swift glance from beneath a fringe of hastily lowered eyelids, caught an assessing

look in his dark eyes. 'What have you been up to,
Arabella, to need such a sum? Gambling? Fast cars?'
There could even have been a hint of amusement
lurking somewhere at the back of his voice.

'No.' Her voice was pitched so low that he had to
incline his head, and from the corner of his eye she
saw him move away from the wall, towards the
corner of the velvet sofa on which she sat. 'No, not
even fast men.' What on earth had made her say
anything so utterly tasteless?

He had turned away, intent on grinding out his
cigarette in a crystal ashtray, making it impossible for
her to gauge any reaction to her stupid remark, and
when he faced her again his expression was as
impassive as ever, in spite of the restrained violence
in his gesture.

'So . . . why do you want so much money?' There
was a faint curl at his lips. 'Especially when I know
you are the daughter of a very rich man.'

'I was.' Her head dropped, and she studied the
pink fingernails of her folded hands. 'Once I was the
daughter of a rich man, but my father lost all his
money.'

'So . . .' His appraising tone brought her head up
in an indignant jerk. He sounded as if her words
brought him some satisfaction, but his face did not
reinforce that impression. 'So now, Arabella, you are
a poor girl, working for her living?' The glance he
cast over her expressed doubt even more cogently
than his normally sardonic expression.

'That's exactly what I am.' Defiantly she raised her
chin. No matter what he thought, she refused to
allow herself to be patronised. Once she had allowed
it, when she had been too young, too unsure of
herself, too dazzled by the Rudi Schlegel she had
known then to contradict him. In those days, she
thought with increased bitterness, he had patronised
her because she was rich; now he was trying to do
the same because she was no longer rich, and . . .

'A poor girl up to her ears in debt, it would seem.' The words, uttered in a dry tone, broke into her thoughts.

'So'—it was impossible for her to conceal her sarcasm; she forgot her anxiety to help her father and allowed bitterness to show through—'you've put me into a category without hearing the whole story. Now,' she reached out for the handbag lying on the seat beside her, 'it's growing late; I ought to be going home.' Some devil seemed determined to control her tongue. 'Kulu will begin to worry if . . .'

'Damn Kulu!' The words which formed so often in Arabella's mind burst from him in suppressed fury, and he grabbed her arm as she rose, forcing her back on to the settee and sinking down beside her, his hard fingers continuing to cut into her flesh. 'You are right, Arabella.' With an effort he controlled himself and spoke more persuasively than he had done all evening. 'I really ought not to jump to conclusions.' Even his brief smile, a dazzle of white against the darkness of his skin, threatened her, made her long to soften against him, to persuade the years to melt away, to regain the bewildering joy they had once known together. But as if he had some direct insight to her thoughts, his fingers slackened, released her abruptly. 'Tell me, Arabella.' Another sudden stomach-jerking smile. 'I promise not to interrupt.'

Swiftly, without looking at him, she told the story, beginning with the first shattering telephone call the other night, finishing with the second frantic call just a few hours earler. Quite deliberately she avoided any details of the first crash, the disaster she had had to face all those years ago after his desertion. When he ought to have been by her side, helping, protecting her.

'So that's it.' She shrugged. 'That's why I'm so worried. And showing it, if what all my friends tell me is true.' Deliberately she placed her hand on her bag. 'The thing is . . .' Her throat was suddenly

convulsed with tears, words stuck in her throat.
' . . .Dad had a heart attack some years ago. If he
doesn't unload his business worries pretty soon, then
I'm sure he'll be heading for another. And of course
he's older now, and . . .'

'You're very fond of him, aren't you, Arabella?'

'Of course.' She adored her father, wildly, unreason-
ably, but that was an admission she was not prepared
to use. Not yet . . .

'And your mother, she is dead, of course.'

'You know she is.' Years ago he had sympathised
that she had never known her mother, so why did he
have to ask?

'Yes, I know.' He spoke flatly, then with an abrupt
change became businesslike. 'But what about your . . .
employer? I would have thought he was the natural
person to turn to at a time like this.'

'Oh, Kulu . . .' Certainly she wasn't going to tell
him she had already drawn a blank there. 'Kulu has
business worries of his own right now. The recession
has hit everyone in the rag trade, and perhaps top
designers most of all. But anyway. I'm sure things
will turn out all right. Now', she glanced at her
watch, 'I really must get home, so . . .'

With a swift move Rudi rose, going again to the
silver box on a side table and lighting a cigarette.
Arabella got to her feet and waited, knowing by
some instinct that his next words would be important.
Her heart was thumping painfully against her ribs,
her mouth was dry, tongue clinging to the roof of her
mouth. And she waited. It was as if he, too,
understood the significance of what he was about to
suggest, and understanding it, was determined to
weigh his words with extreme care. But at last his lips
moved; he was frowning as he gazed at the cigarette
he held in front of him, not even looking at her.

'I am prepared to give you the money, Arabella . . .
under certain circumstances.'

'You . . .' It wasn't entirely artifice which made her

subside on to the couch. Her knees had weakened so
suddenly that quite simply they were unable to
support her weight. It had all been so easy, perhaps
too easy, and yet . . . Certain circumstances. What
on earth could he mean? 'But I couldn't possibly
allow you to . . .' Here she was, all innocence, acting
as if it hadn't been planned, or half planned at the
very least, since that very first suggestion from Kulu.
Maybe even before that . . .

'Why couldn't you allow it?' Now he was studying
her with an air of cynical scepticism which brought a
flare of guilty colour to her cheeks.

'Because . . .' she stammered, 'why on earth should
you? It isn't as if you *know* my father. He might just
be a confidence trickster, or someone who's so
hopelessly inefficient that he ought not to be trusted
with . . .' Her voice trailed away when she realised
that was exactly how her father must appear to
someone like Rudi Schlegel . . .

'I wouldn't be doing it for him.' He cut into her
dismal thoughts. 'I would be doing it for you,
Arabella.' His voice was almost tender.

'For . . . me?' For a second she could hardly
believe that she had actually heard him speak the
words; there was even a momentary conviction that
her brain was playing tricks, making her hear the
words simply because they were the ones she longed
for. But they were still ringing in her ears, so she
knew she had made no mistake. A wave of pure joy
raced through her, tormenting, delighting . . .

'Yes.' It took just a few seconds to realise that
Rudi gave no sign of sharing her feelings, that his
reactions were as matter-of-fact and businesslike as if
he were a tycoon about to enter into some risky
negotiations. 'And only, Arabella,' at last he raised
his eyes, looking at her so dominatingly that she felt
like a rabbit in thrall to a stoat, 'if you agree to
become my wife.'

There was another moment of such intense dizzying

pleasure that she couldn't think straight. Tears of joy
pricked at her eyes, and she blinked them away,
warned by some vague instinct that the time for self-
indulgent weeping had not yet come. Indeed, Rudi
seemed just then to be in a mood unreceptive towards
feminine weakness. Yet he had spoken the words she
had dreamed of for so many years; he wanted to
marry her, that could mean one thing only . . .

'But,' it was her own voice, distant, disembodied,
successfully concealing her own feelings, 'but why,
Rudi? Why should you want to marry me?'

'Why?' His grin was so unexpected that she was on
the verge of relaxing sufficiently to respond, but the
smile was gone as quickly as it had come. 'Because
no one would give such a sum without some kind of
collateral. Your father would not expect it otherwise,
and . . .'

Pain! When had contact with him ever meant
anything else? Now it engulfed her like an avalanche.
She raised her chin defiantly as she snatched the
words from him.

'. . . And he most certainly would not agree to it!
He would much rather face the consequences of his
own misjudgments than expect me to make the
sacrifices.' Probably her choice of that word was
instinctive, like her need to hit back at him. She
shook with self-disgust; how could she have made the
mistake of thinking . . . oh, what was she doing here,
for heaven's save? Had she really planned all this,
schemed to get him to offer the money which would
save her father?

'Of course he would.' Smoothly Rudi interrupted
her thoughts so she had to struggle to recall what he
meant. 'You, on the other hand, would hate it for
him. You would much prefer to make the sacrifice'—
yes, he remembered the word; his voice dwelt on it
scornfully—'than to see him go to prison. Am I not
right, Arabella, in thinking it might come to that?'

'I don't for a minute imagine it would. He has

many friends who will be able, will *want* to help him.'
The eyes looking at him filmed over, and he became
a mere shivery outline. Abruptly she turned and
walked to the door. 'I . . . I don't suppose there's
any hope of persuading you to change your mind?
Anything else I could do . . .' Her eyes were indicating
explicitly what she meant, but she saw his lips tighten,
and he shook his head in a brief absolute way.

'I think my terms are reasonable enough.'

Arabella drew one shuddering breath. 'I see.
Well . . . I think I'd better go. It's getting late. Thank
you for the offer, but . . .'

'But?' Before she could place her hand on the
knob he had reached her, his fingers closing about
her wrist in a grasp that was immediately arresting.
Inwardly she quivered, but at least his touch had the
effect of banishing her inclination to cry. Fiercely she
faced him, saw his lips move. 'Don't go, Arabella.' A
ripple of feeling ran down her spine—surely it couldn't
be fear? 'Not until we've discussed the matter more
fully.'

'As far as I'm concerned there's nothing to discuss.
It was kind of you to make the offer, but the
conditions are unacceptable. What possible reason
could there be for either of us to embark on such a
marriage?' She forced a laugh between frozen lips.
'Just because once, years ago, we had a stupid little
romance, why should marriage now be such a good
idea? After all,' her heart was beating with such
agitation she thought he must hear it, 'you changed
your mind then, didn't you? You baled out without a
word of explanation, and . . .'

'Not without a word,' he interrupted. 'I agree that
the circumstances were inopportune; we had quarrelled
bitterly and I had no chance of seeing you again
before I had to go, but in my letter I did explain and
give you Joachim's address where you . . .'

'Letter?' Had he really written a letter, something
which could have saved her from so much pain and

bitterness? Or was it convenient now to pretend . . . 'I didn't receive a letter from you.'

'Arabella?' Now she couldn't miss the concern and consternation on his face. 'Are you certain? I . . .'

'Of course I'm certain!' Her anguish made her waspish. 'It isn't, after all, the kind of thing one can be uncertain about.' Sensing that he was about to put a hand up to her cheek, she drew back a step, releasing a shuddering breath that controlled her desire to burst into tears.

'Well . . .' When he spoke again she sensed a withdrawal. 'I suppose what happened so long ago is hardly relevant now. Memories can become clouded over the years . . . But to answer your question, I think it would be a good idea, because we're both much more sensible people than we were then. I like you, Arabella,' he might have been speaking of one of the dresses in Kulu's collection. 'And I've never forgotten you. I'm thirty-one and it's time I married. I'm a rich man, rich enough to guarantee that you'll always be able to have what you want.'

'Oh . . .' it was very nearly a sob. 'If what I wanted was money then I could have married years ago, but people don't get married for reasons like that. You don't reach a certain age and say, this year, I must get married.'

'Believe me, there are worse ways of approaching it.' His smile tempted and almost gained a response, but she had the good sense to stifle that inclination. At one time she had been only too willing to fall in with whatever mood or whim he expressed, and look where that had led. Now she was much older, and she hoped, wiser. And besides in his expression there was something . . . a watchfulness, as if her every reaction was being noted, analysed and stored away for future reference. And certainly she had no intention of making it that easy for him.

'And many better ones. No,' she smiled with the same insincerity she imagined was governing his actions, 'thank you, but no. I'm sure my father would have it on his conscience for the rest of his days if I were to ruin my life for his sake.' She chose the words deliberately and watched keenly for a response, but to her disappointment she saw none. Rather, she encountered a softening in his manner, a persuasiveness in his expression which, if it were continued, she would find very difficult to reject.

'But don't you see, *Liebling*?' The endearment, once so familiar, spoken with the ease of long custom and in that caressing, deeply pitched voice, made her heart slip a little from its moorings and her senses reeled under the shock. 'He need never know. I imagine it is not a thing you will wish to confide to anyone, and no one will hear of it from me. All your father need be told is that you are marrying a man who is in a position to help him, that he will be only too happy to do so. If you play your part as well as I'm sure you can, then there's little doubt he'll think it mere happy chance that you fell in love with a rich man. After all, isn't that what most men hope for for their daughters?' The cynicism in his voice was unmistakable, but he was impervious to her stony look. 'Doesn't society think girls have married well only if the men are wealthy or successful?'

'And are you going to tell me that most men don't welcome the opportunity to marry money themselves?' The query, with the faintest stress on one word was out before she could stop it.

'*Most* men,' his eyes narrowed as he took up the emphasis she had chosen, 'perhaps *most* men.' But I am not like most men; his attitude implied, as clearly as he had once stated, that the rules that apply to others are not for Rudi Scchlegel.

As if that wasn't something she knew only too well. Her heart cried out in bitter protest. Why, why, why had she been caught in this trap again? Seeing him, she should have run for her life rather than risk being overwhelmed by his influence. Even now,

inwardly she wept in despair, now that he had asked
her to marry him, she had no idea what he felt for
her. Had he thought of proposing before she had
blurted out the facts of her father's situation? Or had
he made his suggestion on the spur of the moment,
his memory jogged, perhaps even anxious to atone
for his past behaviour? Obviously he couldn't bring
himself to speak about it yet, but . . . Oh, why was
she wasting time going over it all? There were simply
no answers to the questions that teemed in her mind.

'Anyway,' weakly she turned away, ignoring the
fingers still clamped about her wrist, 'there's no point
saying any more about it. There simply is no common
ground, and so there's no point in discussing the
matter. We're just wasting time, yours and mine, and
I would like to go now. Will you take me, or shall I
ring for a taxi?'

'Later, I shall see that you reach the flat safely, but
now, we still have something to discuss.' The pressure
increased and she felt herself being led back into the
room, forced to resume her seat on the long, soft
couch. 'Think, *Liebling*.' He had thrown himself into
the farthest corner, arms extended at right angles
along the back and side, slewed round so he had a
comfortable view of her profile. For she refused to
look at him. At the moment it was the only resistance
open to her. 'Think, *Liebling*, of the advantages
marriage would bring. You would have . . . a house
in the Grünewald.' He paused as if, as *if* she needed
to be reminded of, taunted with her juvenile
aspirations. 'And I have a rather nice house in
Bavaria as well. You could do worse, I suspect.'

'If you imagine I'll be tempted to marry a man just
because I can't resist his property guide then you
know nothing about me.'

'And yet,' his voice was silky smooth, 'once you
expected me to marry you for that very reason.'

'*No!*' In spite of her determination otherwise she
whirled round, making sure he could not miss the

expression of angry contempt on her face. 'No,' she shook her head, feeling the silky drift of hair, 'there was another reason, as I remember.' With the utmost difficulty she suppressed a sob, looking with a wide-eyed desperation for the man she had once known, but finding no reflection in the impassive stare of a man intent on seeking out her weakness. 'Besides,' she forced herself to speak with more control, regretting that she had lowered her guard for an instant, 'you still haven't explained just why you should want to marry. I don't imagine it's simply to help my father with his problems.'

'Very well.' There was a weariness about him, quite at odds with his usual image, and she could have sworn she heard a faint sigh, although again she refused to look at him. But she knew that he was crossing the room again, taking another cigarette from the box, flicking a lighter, and then the sharply indrawn breath, the scent, faintly aromatic, came to her nostrils before he spoke again.

'Quite simply, Arabella, I want to have children.'

The statement, so utterly unexpected, spoken so baldly, made her head jerk upwards, eyes wide to look at him, leaning so casually against the mantelpiece, surveying her with that unwinking gaze. Now, in conjunction with his words, the wave of emotions that swamped her brought colour to her cheeks. 'Wh . . . what did you say?' It was barely a whisper.

'I said I would like to have children while I'm still young enough to enjoy them.' There was a curl at the corners of his mouth, almost inviting her to join in a joke at his expense. 'Time is going on, and I don't want to leave it too late.'

'But . . . why me?' It cost her an effort to pose the question. Maybe she was even offering him a second opportunity to tell her what she was longing to know—that he had loved her ever since they had first met, that it had never wavered through all the empty years and that now all he wanted to make his life

perfect was for her to give him the answer he sought.
'Why me?' she repeated as he seemed to hesitate.

'Why not you, Arabella?' Briefly he turned away,
tapping some ash from his cigarette before returning
to view her with the cool detachment which she felt
more keenly than actual dislike. 'I find the thought of
you as my wife one that appeals, and I'm sure you
would make a good mother.'

'Really?' It would have been hard to describe the
effect his words were having; inside she felt bruised,
hurt in a way that was indefinable, and her reaction
was to strike back. 'But what would you say if I told
you that I dislike children and that I have no intention
of having any? Ever. And . . .'

'In that case,' he interrupted with infuriating
detachment, 'of course the offer would be withdrawn,
if I were to be convinced that no persuasions of mine
could alter your point of view.'

Arabella stared at him, unable at first to understand
just what he was meaning, and then when she did,
the wave of anger and disgust she felt made her voice
shake. '. . . And,' she continued, to remind him that
she had been interrupted, 'that if I did want children,
you would be the last man I would choose as their
father.'

If a reaction was what she wanted then she was not
disappointed. With a gesture that was sheer fury he
tossed the cigarette into an ashtray and took a few
steps in her direction. Before she understood what
was happening she found herself jerked to her feet.
One hand beneath her chin held her immobile, giving
her no chance of avoiding the tempest controlling
him just then.

'And yet,' his eyes flashed with slaty brilliance, 'I
seem to remember once we came very close to the
possibility of creating a child. Oh, by accident of
course. And now you tell me . . .'

'That,' she spoke through clenched teeth, 'was

when I was little more than a child myself. Too young to understand what I was doing.'

'You weren't a child, Arabella.' The abrupt change from fury to deliberate persuasiveness caused a shudder to rack her. 'You were a young woman, beautiful, desirable.' The strong fingers holding her chin slackened, moved to circle her throat in a gentle clasp before sliding beneath the fall of hair, pulling her closer so she could feel the warmth of his breath on her skin.

At the same time his other arm came round her, his hand resting lightly about her waist before slipping lower, fingers outspread, bringing their bodies into immediate, intimate contact.

Arabella felt her breathing grow still more agitated. Her heart was beating fiercely against her ribs, and all she could consider was the closeness of his mouth to hers. She was determined she would not submit to him; it would be too easy. Panic mounted as his lips brushed seductively against hers. Her tiny moan was part protest, entire surrender, and she melted against him as her mind spiralled out of control.

It had never been like this with anyone else. Part of her determined to remain detached, as if she were conducting some kind of experiment. Time after time in the intervening years she had struggled to recapture the sheer wonder and magic, but she had never even come close. Her hands, at first trapped between their bodies, moved up and round his neck, her long fingers holding, caressing, cupping his face, then brushing, tangling in his hair while she held his mouth in deepening contact with hers.

'So you see,' abruptly the dream came to an end, her eyelids flicked open, the gentle brown eyes blank with shock as they stared into his cynically amused expression, 'you wouldn't find it all that difficult, Arabella. It's possible you might even find some pleasure in the experience.'

A shaft of sheer anguish pierced through her breast.

and it was with great difficulty that she controlled the bitter retort which rose to her lips. She contented herself with a faint little smile which she hoped he would take for self-possession, at the same time reaching behind for her handbag before returning to look at him, all signs of fury wiped from her features.

'I didn't say I wouldn't *enjoy* the preliminaries, Rudi. I wouldn't be such a fool as to tell such a stupid lie. I dare say we would both find it a pleasant enough way of passing an odd hour. What I said was that if ever I decide to have a child, *you* will not be the father. And now . . .'

'You little . . .' His finger bit again into her upper arms, and she knew that her skin would bear the marks in the morning. The detached, professional part of her was grateful that the show was over. Coolly she looked into the blazing fury of his face, a tiny thrill of triumph rising inside her, dispelling the ache for a moment as she realised that she possessed a very potent means of undermining his detachment. He gave her a final shake before releasing her with a contempt that just stopped short of throwing her aside.

'I'll have the car brought round.' He stalked from the room, and a few seconds later she heard the distant sound of his voice in conversation with the chauffeur. Then he was back, standing inside the door briefly before walking forward, appearing behind her in the mirror which she now faced. Fiddling with her earring gave her the excuse to ignore him until the dominant pull of his expression became too much and she looked straight into his eyes.

'Ernst will be round immediately.'

'Oh? Thank you.' A blink dispelled the wash of tears.

'And . . .' in the mirror she watched his dark fingers come up to touch the white cotton of her blouse, '. . . think about what I said, Arabella. I'm sure we could be . . . content.'

'I really can't understand you.' Refusing to allow his gentler mood to undermine her bitterness, she withdrew her arm deliberately. 'If you want to marry, to have a family, why don't you choose someone else, someone like Fräulein Steyr? After all, you and she must have everything in common.'

'Ah, Klara.' His tone was reflective, very nearly melancholy. 'Don't you know, people in that sort of world always put their careers first? Husbands might be tolerated but families, especially children, just don't figure.'

Again that feeling of a weapon being thrust deep into her breast. The words she spoke were what she was feeling. 'So, just because she refuses, you have chosen me.' But at least she had been able to wipe off the bitterness, was even able to touch her reply with amused condescension.

He made no reply, but his hand on her arm guided her to the door. 'Think about it, Arabella. I still can bring to mind no one whom I'd rather have as the mother of my children. Including Klara.'

'How kind.' she smiled insincerely. 'May I let you know?'

'I would, of course'—for some reason she could not explain, her stupid remark appeared to annoy him—'want proof that you were not already pregnant.'

The words echoed round her skull, and she felt the colour drain from her face as they reached the front door. But she turned to face him, determined to cope with the desperation that made her long to weep.

'I see.' How controlled and calm she sounded. 'You mean you would like a medical certificate?'

'No. Your word would be sufficient.'

'Don't trouble to come with me.' She dismissed him. 'I'll make do with Ernst.' And she ran down the steps, past the uniformed man who was holding the car door for her. And she spared not a single glance for the figure outlined against the open doorway, for

the man who for the second time in her life had
wounded her beyond endurance.

But still she couldn't repress a tiny frisson of
remorse. For just a few moments she had held her
father's salvation in her hands, until remembered
bitterness had made her toss it aside. She suspected
that was an indulgence she would live to regret, and
worse still, the cruel words she had thrown at Rudi
did nothing to enhance her own opinion of herself.
Rather the reverse.

Wearily she got out of the car and took the lift to
the second floor, her mind still whirling round in
desperate circles. But no matter how she struggled,
she could think of no one else who was in a position
to help. Always her instincts seemed to lead her back
to one man. Oh, how she *wished* they had never met!

CHAPTER FOUR

IT HAD all been so romantic, meeting Rudi Schlegel that first long-ago summer in Berlin. And being singled out by him would have gone to the head of any inexperienced eighteen-year-old; for Arabella it was intoxication of the most potent, delicious kind.

'Very soon I return to Berlin. You must come with me.' So he had decreed within days of their meeting, and she hadn't for an instant stopped to consider the inherent risks of abandoning her only friends in a strange country to follow a man she didn't know. For of course by then she felt she had loved him for ever.

Everything about him was different; beside him all her other friends of the opposite sex were callow and gauche. And it wasn't all to do with age; certainly he was older than her usual escorts, but about him hung a faint air of mystery, a suggestion of suffering in spite of his civilised, friendly manner. There were times, when they were sitting among the crowds collected round tables at the outdoor cafés, when he seemed miles away from the frequently juvenile chatter, remote until a direct remark brought his attention back from which ever dark recess it had found. Yes, she couldn't deny that there was something about him she didn't understand, which intrigued her, and which she was confident that she alone would help him to overcome.

That was why she found it so easy to respond to his invitation. There was no need even to consider it; she had simply to follow her instincts. There was no point in anyone trying to dissuade her; the only advice she would listen to was that she wanted to hear. Certainly the restrained warnings of Ernst and his parents had gone unheeded. It wasn't as if she knew them particularly well either. They were relatives of an employee of her father, who had agreed to have her as a paying guest just to oblige him.

And it wasn't that they had anything against Rudi, just that they didn't know enough about him to allow her to go without question. But a quick and not altogether frank telephone call to her father had gained his permission, rather more easily than Arabella had expected, though the reasons for that became clear only much later. At the time she had no suspicion that he had more on his mind than the normal troubles of running a huge property empire.

So she followed Rudi to Berlin and settled happily into the small flat he found for her. Well, it was more of a bedsit than a flat, with a bed that swung up against the wall during the day, leaving just enough room for two chairs and a tiny table. A large cupboard had been transformed into a kitchen where she could play at cooking, and an even smaller shower room completed the mod cons. It wasn't cheap, but even so, her allowance would have stretched to something much more ambitious, only she hadn't yet revealed to Rudi that she was the daughter of a very rich man. That news she was saving for a special occasion, happily hugging to herself the pleasure he would feel when he knew.

From almost the first he had told her with wondering delight that he loved her, and before they had known each other a month that he wanted to marry her. 'You see, *mein Schätzchen*'—unusually they were spending an evening in his flat, similar to her own but slightly bigger with a bedroom as well as a sitting-room—'always I thought I would not marry. I could never imagine a woman who could persuade me to give up my freedom.' His hands held her face, raising her mouth close to his. 'But the moment I saw you sitting with that Ernst Fischer in Willi's *Bierhalle*'—when he spoke the name his mouth trembled with laughter—'such a romantic spot, *nicht wahr*? Willi's *Bierhalle*,' he teased as if the spot had been of her choosing. 'When we tell our children that is where we met, what do you think they will say?'

'I can't imagine.' She was learning to appear a bit more blasé, to hide from him the devastating effects of such comments. The thought that one day, and in the not too distant future, she might have his child . . .

'You think your father will approve of me? Will he like the idea of losing his only child to a stranger?'

'He won't mind.' The very idea of her father refusing her anything made her smile. 'And your parents, do you think they'll approve of me?'

'How could they resist?' But he quickly turned the conversation away from that; he rarely spoke of his family except to tell her that his father and mother lived in the Eastern Zone. Behind the hideous Wall. It was easy to understand just how painful he would find it.

So the days passed, and with each of them she sank more deeply in love with him. Looking back, it was as if she had spent those weeks in a little girl's dream, in a kind of fairytale divorced from reality with Rudi as the handsome prince, although it was hard to equate the strength of her feelings with anything childish. But when she woke up from the dream it was to find her world in ruins about her.

An evening or two later they had gone for a walk in the Grünewald, intending to join some friends for beer and sausages in one of the *Gasthäuser* scattered through the forest, but in the meantime savouring the pleasures of being on their own and the delights of planning their future together.

When they reached a grassy knoll deep in the wood it seemed natural for them to sink down, arms about each other, faces, mouths coming together as if that was the natural way of things. Then Rudi was murmuring against her cheek all those tender words which had played no part in her study of the language and which were so all important.

'*Liebchen*,' he was outlined starkly against the chequered canopy of leaves, sun slanted at a low angle touching with gold the long sweep of his lashes, 'when shall we be married? I cannot wait much longer. It is torture to be with you like this.' One hand slipped beneath her breast, and he smiled at the rapid tattoo of her pulse. 'I too feel it . . . See . . .' And taking her hand he placed it in the open front of his shirt, where she could feel the spring of silky hair before moving on to the taut warmth of his skin and the echo of her own fevered emotions.

'Let's go.' Abruptly he was frowning; with one lithe move he had risen and was looking down at her. He was pushing his shirt more securely into the waistband of his jeans, then was offering a hand to pull her to her feet. And Arabella, bewildered by the sudden change in him, hurt by the abrupt descent from near bliss to everyday reality, felt her lip tremble for a second before she caught it in her teeth.

'All right,' she tossed her head back, smiled but with a shade too much brilliance, 'let's.' Unable to bear the brooding expression, she made a fuss of brushing pieces of straw and sand from her printed cotton skirt. 'Otherwise,' and now her annoyance could scarcely be controlled, 'we shall keep Gretl and Wolfie waiting.'

'*Ja.*' They walked on opposite sides of the path till they had almost reached their rendezvous when Rudi crossed without her noticing, swinging her round to face him. 'Forgive me.' All the blackness had been wiped from his face, had been replaced by a sad, almost a haunted expression which caught at her heart.

'Nothing to forgive.' Standing a little on tiptoe, she brushed his mouth with hers in a way he found irresistible.

'There is,' he insisted huskily. 'Some day I shall be able to explain . . .'

'Hi, you two.' Wolfgang was standing on the edge of the clearing waving to them, his voice shattering the stillness of the warm evening. '*Komm—schnell*! We have been waiting.'

And during the rest of the evening Rudi's dark eyes were sending messages over the top of his *Bierstein*. 'Forgive me,' he was saying, and her soft expression must have given him the answer he sought. In fact by the time they were wandering, arms entwined, back through the darkening but still busy streets to her flat, Arabella decided that there was nothing half so sweet in life as coming together after the mildest of tiffs. How she could cope with a monumental one she could not envisage. But the very next evening she was to find out.

They had spent some hours wandering down the Kurfürstendamm, following the set pattern of that time and place, lingering among the pavement stalls with their displays of cheap jewellery, stopping frequently so that Arabella could study a particularly fascinating window. And Rudi would smile as usual, although possibly with a shade more abstraction than she liked, as if her admiration of the exotic and highly priced clothes were a joke, a dream unlikely to be realised.

'Wait till I write my bestselling novel,' he advised, 'then you shall have whatever you like.'

'Oh, yes?' She raised a teasing eyebrow, her manner coyly determined to keep her secret for just a little longer. 'But what if I'm not prepared to wait until I'm an old woman to be able to buy a dress like that?' She waved a hand towards the pale blue silk creation draped across a spindly gilt chair. 'I would like to own some decent clothes while I'm still young enough to enjoy them.'

'Then,' he paused to grasp her upper arm, holding her so still among the hurrying crowds that she was forced to notice the edgy pulse beating at one corner of his mouth, the expression of tense anxiety in his eyes, 'I shall just have to step up the production, shan't I?' The lightness of his tone was trying to conceal his real mood. 'And you must simply ensure that our home life is so placid that I'll be able to dash it off in a couple of months.'

'Oh,' she eased herself into the curve of his arms, wishing she could find the right words to wipe the strain from his face, 'maybe I'll be able to buy my own dresses.'

'No, don't spoil that for me.' The kiss he dropped on to her cheek made her want to burst into tears. 'I'm the kind of man who has to provide those things for my wife. Besides, it won't be for long. Already I have most of the book in my head. All ready.' Then he stopped as if with a sudden inspiration. 'You can't type, I suppose.'

'I'm afraid not.' Disappointment at being unable to fulfil such a simple task made her disregard his initial declaration. 'You must just take me as I am.' Again there was a suggestion of smug secrecy.

'I'll do just that.' The wide *Platz* around the Kaiser Wilhelm Kirche lay before them and they flopped on to a vacant seat where they had an uninterrupted view of the bomb-scarred building with its striking modern rotunda. Rudi turned to face her, pulling her close, signalling his ownership, catching a strand of her hair and twisting it round one finger. 'That's what I want most in all the world. I suppose,' his sigh, the lengthening silence made her heart beat in unexplained agitation until he went on, 'soon we shall have to think of your father. Can you be certain he won't object to his darling child marrying a German, coming to live in this threatened city?'

Arabella shrugged, wishing she could thrust aside the need to face up to any such problems. 'That seems to be the last thing you think of on an evening like this. It's all so perfect. Too peaceful for one to think of threats.'

'*Ja.*' Now the bitterness which she had sensed all evening was unmistakable. 'The façade can be very convincing at times. But look around you.' He flicked a glance towards the memorial church and she wished she had been less superficial, but before she had time to dwell on that he continued in a more cheerful voice. 'Do you think your father will mind you living in a tiny flat? Perhaps,' he considered briefly, 'we might just be able to afford something a little bigger. Just,' his white teeth gleamed suddenly and Arabella's heart flipped over, ''till I get the novel published you understand.'

'Of course.' Although she was willing to join in the game, her wonderful secret was too urgent to be withheld any longer. 'But I *do* think Daddy might prefer to see his darling child,' her repetition of his words was self-mocking, 'in something a bit better than the flat. Say, something like one of those villas we passed this evening. On the way to the Grünewald?' She slid a glance in his direction, dropping her eyes suddenly to hide their mischievous expression.

'*Ja.*' He was tolerant, amused now, but much more involved with his fingers on the back of her neck than with her game. His touch made excitement rise inside her. Married to him and living in one of those gorgeous houses—she had even noticed a swimming pool in one of the gardens. She had a tantalising glimpse of herself presiding over the household; perhaps they could make do with just one maid; she meant to learn to cook, so . . .

'*Ja*, one day perhaps.' He was being indulgent, travelling with her to the Never-Never-Land and with no idea of the wonderful surprise she was preparing.

'I think,' turning to him, she played for a moment with the top buttons of his shirt before allowing the back of her hand to lie there, against the warm skin, 'if I ask him nicely, Daddy might give us a house like that for a wedding present.'

'But of course.' Still he was enjoying the joke, then, seeing her wide-eyed expression, her words suddenly lost their humour, gained more significance, and his smile faded abruptly. It was clear that the implication of her words was beginning to make sense. 'Arabella?' Eyes narrowed, amusement was wiped from his features as if by a duster and suddenly she was nervous, afraid, as if she were dealing with an alien being.

Only determined self-confidence could help her now, and that was the manner she assumed. 'If I ask him, I know Daddy will give us a villa so we can start our married life in style. After all,' her faint laugh rang with uncertainty, 'there's no virtue in being uncomfortable if you don't have to. Is there?' Appealing eyes were raised to his. 'Is there?'

'Are you telling me your father will not want you to marry if we have to start our lives in a manner I can afford?'

'No, all I'm saying is that there's no need.' Confidence was seeping back; he would be unable to deny the sense of what she was saying. 'No need for us to live in that grotty little flat'—that word was a mistake, she knew it the instant it issued from her lips but she blundered on—'my father is quite able to buy us a house.'

'I thought you said your father was a builder.' He frowned with the effort of remembering her exact words. 'A builder in a small way, I think you said.'

'Yes, I did. That's just a joke. He calls himself that, but . . .' A chill, in defiance of the warmth of the night entered the very marrow of her bones.

'But . . .' he insisted cruelly.

'But that's how he started.' The words burst from her. 'After the war he used his gratuity to start out on his own as a builder. And he was successful.'

'How successful?'

'Quite successful.' It was iniquitous that she was being subjected to the third degree just because her father had been successful, and she couldn't see why she had to apologise. If he had failed, gone bust, then maybe . . . Her chin rose slightly, and she returned his look of cold enquiry with one that was stormy but defiant. 'He's one of the most important property developers in the country— Gordon Smythe Holdings.' The name was one she usually spoke with pride; how dared he try to rob her of some of that?

'Gordon Smythe Holdings.' There was a certain note in his voice, not quite a sneer perhaps, but abruptly he allowed his hand to drop from her neck, at the same time and without appearing to move, increasing the distance between them so she was aware of total rejection. Wordlessly she saw him extract a cigarette from his shirt pocket, watched him light it with a match flicked by his thumbnail then draw smoke deep into his lungs. 'I have heard of them.'

His eyes which had almost invariably regarded her with warmth were now detached and . . . neutral. Inwardly Arabella shivered but at the same time she was consumed with anger. With him? With herself? She didn't know, but she regretted the haste with which she had allowed herself to spring the surprise. But why should she be apologetic with what was surely good news? He, after all, expected her to be delirious at the prospect of the fortune he would derive from his book. A book that he hadn't even begun writing. She tried to express her feelings, struggled to be tactful.

'Yes, they're a fairly well-known company. I think my father's the kind of man you would admire. In his own way he's done what you plan to do.'

'Yes?' His tone told her that that viewpoint he rejected.

'Yes.' His brevity stung as much as his manner. 'It's all right for you to talk about making a lot of money, wrong apparently for him to have done it.' She pushed herself away from him, to the furthest edge of the seat, looking with angry eyes at the people wandering across the square, finding one pair of uninhibited lovers particularly trying.

'What I'm trying to say is,' he made no move to close the gap between them, 'that when I marry I shall expect, no, I'll insist on supporting my own wife; I shall not accept subsidies from her father. What I have we shall share, but until I can provide the luxuries she will live at my level. Even,' now his voice was heavy with sarcasm, 'even if all I can provide for her is a grotty flat.'

'Doesn't that strike you,' tears were stinging at her eyes, 'as just a bit old-fashioned and . . . selfish?'

He shrugged his indifference to other viewpoints. 'That is how I am.'

'How very convenient and complacent!' Arabella felt her temper boil over quite suddenly; she got to her feet and stood looking down at him, her voice sufficiently raised to attract the passers-by. One old man walking his dog even stood, regarding them with amazed fascination, his head moving from one side to the other as if he were at a tennis match, but neither of them noticed. 'What you're saying is,' firmly she repressed a sob but her eyes were ablaze, 'I'm the one who must make all the sacrifices and . . .'

'Sacrifices?' He pounced on the word like a terrier on a rat. 'Sacrifices, did you say?' His eyes narrowed and he got to his feet slowly but with an air of menace. Arabella wished with all her heart that she could look elsewhere, but his expression of cold dislike fascinated. Fascinated and frightened. She licked dry lips, wishing she could recall the obnoxious word. But on the other hand it was true; it was she who was expected to give up everything while he . . . 'I did not realise you considered marriage to me in that light . . .'

'I didn't say I considered our marriage a sacrifice.' She found herself speaking through clenched teeth— it was the only way she could retain some control but afterwards she wondered if it had made her look and sound quite ugly, almost vicious.

'What, then? What did you mean?' His manner suggested he would be difficult to convince.

'I'm saying,' a deep breath was intended to calm, 'that there are sacrifices to be made, but they're all on one side. If you could make a small sacrifice, relax your principles a bit,' in spite of all her effort and determination a hint of sarcasm lingered in her voice, 'then we could begin our married life in some degree of comfort.'

'You brought up the subject of sacrifice.' His eyes, normally so soft and warm, so admiring, could look horribly cold and unfriendly, like wet slate. 'Tell me, please, what are these sacrifices which have been so much on your mind?'

'I didn't say they had been on my mind. Why do you twist everything? But I should have thought they were fairly apparent to any intelligent person. One,' she began ticking off on her fingers, 'I was going to university in October, but I'm giving that up for you. It will be a great disappointment to my father; it's what he's always planned for me. Two,

I'm having to leave my family and friends—I do have some, you know.'

'As to that, there is a perfectly good university here: Berlin's Freie Universität is not unknown—is one of the best in Europe, I should have thought. As to family and friends—well, I thought I was to be your family, and already you have made friends. Berlin is two or three hours from London, closer than many places in the United Kingdom. A very minor sacrifice, I suggest.'

'I *was* prepared to make them.' Passionately she defended herself. 'Gladly. But . . . I still can't see why you won't make one for me. In fact, most people wouldn't think it much of a sacrifice, being given an attractive house to live in. Most men would thank their lucky stars that their father-in-law was in the position to help . . . Most men . . .'

'I am not most men.' He interrupted with what she considered blatant bad manners. 'I am Schlegel. And I will not be someone else just so we can live in some kind of luxury we have not earned.'

'How very fine and liberal!' she sneered, angered by his dictatorial style. 'It's as I said: you're the one with the principles, I'm the one who makes the sacrifices.'

'You . . .' The tender loving mouth was little more than a thin line as he bit off an epithet, the fingers which could caress so tenderly could be hard and cruel. 'If you imagine for a moment I'm going to be some kind of kept man'—a quick shake emphasised his words—'some kind of gigolo, then you are much more stupid than I thought you were.' Afterwards she couldn't decide whether he had been shouting at the top of his voice, letting Berlin and the world know exactly what he thought of her. Or was it just that the words, the contemptuous message, was seared on to her brain?

Much more stupid . . . This was the man she loved, who loved her and wanted to marry her . . .

She was numb with shock and despair. Stood looking up into his face and even the slow fading of his anger failed to bring any warmth to her chilled spirit.

'Look, Arabella, this is foolish. We're both saying things . . .' She saw the white teeth bite on the lower lip, was struck as ever by the contrast with tanned skin. 'We'd better leave things there.'

In a dream she saw his hand go up to summon a cruising taxi, watched the vehicle pull in to the footpath. In the same dream she crossed and climbed into the back seat. Rudi spoke to the driver, gave a spate of instructions which ended with the address of her flat, and she saw him pass over a handful of coins without appreciating the significance of the action.

'Goodnight, Arabella.' His head came briefly towards her but there was no farewell kiss; the door banged and the car drew away. She gave a pathetic little whimper, knelt on the sagging leather of the seat and saw his figure, immaculate and striking in the jeans and shirt which, despite being the uniform of the day, he always invested with his own distinction.

'Rudi,' she murmured, wiping away tears with the back of her hand. For she was suddenly terrified that he hadn't said 'Goodnight'. Had his actual words been, 'Goodbye, Arabella'? Once considered, it was impossible for her to rid herself of the suspicion—no, more than that, the certainty—that the brief passionate affair was over and she was seeing Rudi Schlegel for the last time.

Next morning, after a night of weeping, that conviction faded from her mind, and only the pain of their quarrel remained. It had been bitter, but she knew that when he had had time to think of it Rudi would realise the truth of what she had said. He was *bound* to recognise that at least some of the right had been on her side. And when he came round to make up the quarrel she would give in gracefully, would confess that after all she didn't want to live in one of those grand houses in the Grünewald; they were for the middle-aged and stodgy. No, what she would really like was a nice modern flat somewhere close to the lakes, a modest little place so as not to offend Rudi's sensibilities, but with a spare bedroom for her father when he came over to visit. And of course none of the other things would be a sacrifice. Or at least if they were, she was happy, longing to make them.

Almost contentedly she pottered round the flat in the forenoon, and after lunch she went to the library to do some reading. Since she was going to be living here, it was essential that she improve her German; becoming fluent in the language must be her first aim.

When Rudi did not turn up that evening it was a disappointment, until she remembered that the previous week he had warned her that he might have to go off to Hanover to do a story. She imagined that must be what had happened; he would be away overnight and tomorrow evening their reunion would be all the sweeter after their separation.

Only, the following night passed with no sign of Rudi, and Arabella, who had been in a state of rising tension for the greater part of the day was numbed, drained of feeling. Of course it was all a coincidence; something must have happened to delay him, and there was no telephone where he could easily contact her. But at the back of her mind a single word was insistent, refusing to go away. Goodbye. More and more she was convinced he had said goodbye, not goodnight. But surely . . . Blank panic was reflected each time she looked in the mirror. Panic and misery so powerful that at ten that night she rushed out into the streets where she picked up a taxi to take her down the Ku'damm.

But this was one evening when all Rudi's friends appeared to have gone to ground en masse. Arabella went to all the various bars where they regularly sat with small glasses of beer, nibbling at sausages while they put the world to rights. But she didn't see a single face that she knew, and gave up the search in the early hours only when an insistent drunk followed her out into the street, determined she should accept his proposition. Luckily a taxi came cruising round the corner at that exact moment and she was able to escape. But when she got home she lay fully clothed on her bed, unable to weep or sleep, staring into the darkness, wondering what she could do.

In the morning she went round to Rudi's flat, all pride banished, simply longing to find him so she could beg his forgiveness. As she sat in the bus which jerked and shuddered its way along the streets she imagined the tenderness with which they would make up their quarrel. So immersed was she in her daydream that she almost passed her stop and it was only the driver's shouted 'Neuköln' which brought her back to the present, and she jumped off before the automatic doors banged shut.

As she ran up the two flights of stairs, her heart was bounding against her ribs, and when she stood with her finger on the doorbell she was weak and shaking. And yet there was no sound at all from inside the flat, nothing except the ringing on the other side of the heavy wooden door. Despair suddenly blotted out her anticipation, and she sobbed, lay with her head against it, fists banging against the panels.

It was only the sound of a door slamming on the upper floor and footsteps running lightly down that made her bite her lips fiercely, search in her bag for a tissue.

'Guten Tag.' Rudi's neighbour, a student to whom she had been briefly introduced paused, the dark

admiring glance doubtless seeing the tears hovering
on the ends of her long lashes. '*Ach*, it is
Fräulein . . . Smythe, *nicht wahr*?' He grinned at
his own cleverness in remembering her name, then
his expression changed as he took in the quivering
lips. 'Something is wrong, *Fräulein*?'

'No, of course not. I just trapped my finger.' She
put her hand briefly to her mouth to support the
story. 'I'm looking for Rudi.'

'Rudi?' He frowned. 'But . . .'

'But . . . you know where I can find him?'

'But, *Fräulein* . . . You did not know?'

'Know?' Feelings of dread wiped out every other
emotion. 'Know what?'

'I am sorry, *Fräulein*, I imagined you would have
known. Rudi has gone back to the Zone, this is
what I have been told. I should think that by this
time he is in Wittenberg. Back with his family, you
understand. *Fräulein*, are you all right?'

'Yes.' Arabella fought the inclination to allow
reality to drift away. There was nothing to be
gained by fainting here, in front of this pleasant
young man whose expression was telling her all too
clearly how much he would like to catch her should
she collapse. 'It was just that I had a . . . book I
want to return to him.' She patted her bag to
confirm her story and even managed a rueful smile.
'But I may as well hang on to it a little longer.'

As they spoke they walked together down the
flights of stairs which gleamed like black polished
marble, emerging at last on to the street, now
sunny enough to suggest the use of tinted glasses.
She pulled them down from the top of her head,
grateful for the small amount of protection they
offered.

'I don't suppose,' it was an afterthought as they
parted to go in opposite directions, 'you have any
idea when Rudi will be back.'

'Back?' Again he looked his surprise. 'But I

understood he would not be coming back, *Fräulein*, that he has left Berlin for good.'

'I see.' She smiled as if she did not care. 'You're probably right. Thank you for your help. *Auf Wiedersehen.*' And with a wave of her hand she turned, walking along so blindly that soon she was well and truly lost.

And all the time, in the unoccupied flat next to the one she had taken, the letter from Rudi which would have explained everything lay gathering dust on the doormat. It was three more months before the owner returned from a visit to Hildesheim, and by then the temporary resident of number 14A had been forgotten.

For another week Arabella waited in Berlin, searching desperately but in vain for anyone who could give her news of what had happened to Rudi Schlegel. And for years afterwards, whenever she met anyone who had a connection with Berlin, the same questions came to her lips. But in all that time she had never had an answer. It was as if Rudi Schlegel had vanished from the face of the earth.

CHAPTER FIVE

'You look ghastly.' Caroline glanced up briefly as Arabella came into the kitchen, and returned to her book before doing a fast double-take. 'Bella!' Her eyes studied her friend as she crossed to the stove and began to pour coffee. 'Are you all right?'

'Fine.' Arabella's voice was thick with a night's crying, the results of which were now impossible to disguise. 'Just . . . I think maybe I've picked up a cold.'

'I didn't really mean it. About you looking ghastly.'

'No.' Arabella's smile was feeble. 'I know, you always say that. Have I ever told you you're a real cat?'

'Often.' Caroline spooned sugar into her cup and stirred morosely. 'It's what they call wearing down the opposition, and as a rule it's the only thing that keeps my spirits up when I see you in the mornings. You always look so disgustingly healthy.'

'Oh, so you *did* mean it!'

'What?'

'Oh, forget it. Tell me, where's the boss?'

'He rushed off to the Schloss to see the Gräfin. Last night she condescended to approve of some of his dresses, and he's dashed off this morning to try to clinch a deal. Evelyn and Naomi are still sleeping it off.'

'They would be. Well, I want to ring home. I'll do it before Kulu gets back, then maybe he won't

80

charge me for the call . . .' Caroline was on her way to the door.

'How did it go last night, Bella? With the dishy man?'

'Oh . . . all right.' There was no chance that she was going to confess to a night's hysterical weeping because of the dishy man. 'We had supper at his house in the Grünewald.'

'Really?' Caroline drifted in pursuit of her friend, lounging against the heavy hall table as Arabella rummaged in her handbag. 'Cosy.'

'What?' There was a feeling of faint warmth on her skin which she hoped would escape Caroline's sharp eye. 'Oh, not really. Do you mind, Caroline?' With one hand covering the receiver, she paused. 'It is a bit private.'

'Of course I don't mind.' Caroline yawned loudly and strolled to the door of her bedroom. 'I think I'll go and make a start on my packing. What time is our flight tonight, can you remember?'

'About ten, isn't it?' Arabella concentrated on dialling. 'I think that's what Kulu said.'

'Good. Gives me time to mooch round the Ku'damm. I want to have a look for some woollens. From what I've heard they're much more reasonable than . . .'

'Hello?' The voice at the other end was one Arabella did not recognise, seeming to belong to a very old man . . .

'Hello. Is that Barway 213064?'

'Arabella!' There was relief in what she now realised was her father's voice, but to hear the ebullient confident man she knew sound so utterly crushed was almost more than she could bear. 'Arabella, how good to hear you, love.'

'Dad.' It was an effort to speak casually. 'How are you? What's been going on since we last spoke?'

'Nothing, my dear.' How very close to breaking point he sounded. 'At least . . . I've handed all my books and papers over to the accountants. Don't worry, it will all turn out well in the end. After all . . . You know me, don't you? Nothing keeps me down for long.'

It was unbearable to listen to him trying to keep going, painful to consider the cost to his pride and self-esteem. Especially when she knew that if she chose . . .

'Look, Dad.' Without giving herself time to consider all the implications she made up her mind. 'I've found someone who's more than willing to put up the money, so you've nothing to worry about. Dad, are you there, can you hear me?'

'Arabella.' The quaver in his voice brought tears stinging to her eyes, and she swallowed, bit her lip. How could she have hesitated for even a second when she was able to bring him such vast relief? 'Arabella, are you sure? It's such a lot of money, and . . .'

'I'm sure, Dad. No problem. It can all be fixed up within a few days . . .'

'Bless you, darling!' Quite subtly his voice had changed, and a little of the habitual bounce and confidence slipped back. 'All along I've felt that something would turn up. But tell me, how have you managed to arrange . . .'

'I can't give you details right now, Dad. You know what I'm like when it comes to high finance, but I'll get Rudi to call you later on. If you can let me know your movements for the rest of the day so he'll be able to contact you.'

'Rudi? Rudi did you say?'

'Yes. Someone I've known for a good many years.' It wasn't the moment to explain that there was a price to be paid for Rudi's help. In any case, she must try to think of things differently—the *reason* for Rudi's willingness to cough up a small fortune. What wealthy man would not pay that price to keep his father-in-law out of prison, to protect the children he planned to have from the indignity of an ex-convict as a grandfather?

Her own cynicism caused a pain in the pit of her stomach, and her lip curled in positive dislike of her father, of herself, of Rudi and the whole sordid, humiliating business. 'I'll ring you later today, Dad. Tell you all about it.'

'Fine.' His increasingly chirpy manner was more for his daughter's peace of mind than for anything else. 'I'll stick around all day in the flat, darling. And thank you.'

'Goodbye, Dad. I'll be in touch.' As she put down the phone Arabella wondered that her father hadn't insisted on knowing just how she had managed to raise so much money in such a short time. He surely knew—none better, she imagined— the difficulties of loans with no security or contacts, and for all he knew she was planning to rob a bank. For the first time in her life she knew a throb of bitter anger against the man whom she had always adored. How *dare* he impose this frightening prospect on her? She began to riffle in her handbag, searching for the small card and telephone number given to her the previous evening, and as she began to dial her mind was completely blank, she heard the ringing tone then his voice answering. Even if she hadn't known who was speaking she would have felt a throb of response to that deep, seductive voice.

'Rudi.' She forgot to identify herself. 'I must see you.'

'Arabella.' There was no surprise; he might have been sitting waiting for her call at—she glanced at her watch—at nine forty-seven exactly. 'I shall be round to pick you up in fifteen minutes.'

He knows. She stared at the telephone as if that object had in some way betrayed her. He probably knew last night, and since then he's been waiting for me to come to heel. How awful . . .

'Bella.' Caroline's head appeared round the door
of her room. 'You finished?' Without waiting for
confirmation she crossed to the bathroom where she
began noisily to collect bottles and jars. 'Your dad
okay?' she enquired as she swept back to her room.

'Fine.' Arabella remembered she had an appointment, shuddering at the possibility that he might
consider that her appearance offered him an excuse
to withdraw from their arrangement. But this was
work at which she was expert. Swiftly she threw off
her T-shirt, kicked herself out of her jeans, her eyes
searching frantically for something suitable for the
awkward occasion that awaited her. A romantic dress
was what she ought to have had to captivate him, but
she hadn't one with her. Anyway, she had no
intention of even trying to do that. If she must she
would marry him; otherwise . . .

Giving the matter no further thought, she snatched
from a hanger she suit she had worn on the journey
out. Probably he was too conventional nowadays to
enjoy seeing a woman wearing man's clothes,
but . . . She pulled on the straight dark trousers,
then boots with stacked heels, struggled into the
frilly white shirt, knotted the wide pink tie. Three
times she had to re-do it before she was satisfied.

Two quick minutes with her make-up, then a
savage thirty seconds with a brush left her hair an
untidy mass of curls. She slipped her arms into the
sleeves of her navy jacket. She looked all right. A
little sombre and businesslike, as the occasion
demanded. It was difficult to explain that last swift
spray of '*Fever*' before she snatched up her shoulder
bag, but then everyone had illogical moments and
she had always loved perfumes. She tried to blot
from her mind that a flacon of that particular
fragrance had been his first, his only gift to her.
That, and the fact that she had stuck with it ever
since.

"Bye.' She encountered Caroline in the hall. 'I don't know when I'll be back.'

'But what shall I tell Kulu?' wailed Caroline before the door banged.

Kulu. As Arabella raced down the stairs, it seemed imperative that she should avoid her employer. He had this utterly unreasonable expectation that his models should be packers and dogsbodies when they weren't actually striding along the catwalks.

'Bella.' With immaculate timing he came through the glass doors of the flat, ignoring the uniformed doorman who held it for him and who continued to hold it wide in expectation that Arabella was making for the street. 'Where on earth are you going?'

'Going?' She cast a glance over his shoulder, understanding just why this situation was one she wanted to avoid. It would be impossible for the two men to meet. 'I have an appointment, Kulu.'

'Bella!' For Kulu the tone of reprimand was mild. 'Didn't it occur to you I'd be depending on your help today?'

'Oh, I'm sure you'll manage.' A silver car drew up at the pavement, and she released her breath as it moved off again. 'Perhaps Caroline and Evelyn will help.' She didn't even have a pang of guilt about the possibility of depriving them of the chance to look round the city.

'Caroline and Evelyn are not you, Bella.' He put an arm about her shoulder. 'You are the only one I can depend on.'

'I have to go, Kulu.' His unusual kindness brought a lump to her throat. 'You *do* understand, don't you?' She placed both hands on his shoulders. 'I have a chance of helping my father, and . . .'

'I see.' He sounded faintly amused. 'You mean you actually took my advice, Bella.'

'What? Oh, of course not.' She shook her head, trying to smile.

'You mean it is *not* Herr von Schlegel you are rushing to meet?' As she shook her head, then nodded, he laughed aloud.

'I'm sure he will be unable to resist you, Bella.' Lightly he linked his arms about her, bent his head to kiss her cheek. 'Off you go, *agapi mou*. Ring if you decide not to come back.'

She was still smiling as she turned and ran from the building, and the first thing she saw was the long silver-grey car. Rudi Schlegel was at the wheel, looking at her with an expression of brooding anger which told her in no uncertain terms that he had seen that meaningless embrace with Kulu. And that he was placing on it the obvious interpretation.

But as she approached he got out of the car and held open the door, slamming it when she slid into the bucket seat, and then took his place at the driving wheel. Since her first tentative smile had been repulsed, Arabella didn't speak, determined that the next approach should come from him.

Stiff with resentment, she sat staring ahead as the long car nosed through the traffic back in the direction of the Grünewald. But though she could not look at him, it was impossible to wipe his picture from her brain where it had been etched by that single glance. He was dressed much more casually than she had yet seen him, wearing a dark blue pullover patterned in large diamonds in red and white, a white shirt collar folded over the crew neckline. And his blue hopsack slacks were remarkably similar to the blue jeans he used to wear. In fact . . .

A sudden thought, a recollection made her hold his breath. Was it her imagination that in the neck of his pullover he had tucked a cornflower? Impossible. He was the least sentimental man she had ever known, and yet . . . Her attempt to focus on the windscreen failed, and she spared a swift sideways glance. Yes. Yes, it was there, and . . .

she drew a sudden sharp breath as she caught sight of another tiny flower tossed into the cubbyhole on his side. So, what did that mean?

'Did he object very much?' Her look had been intercepted, but his manner was discouraging.

'Who?' When she chose, when she was forced to it, she could be as condescending as anyone, so she took no trouble to make her query even faintly polite, but she turned so she could see him more comfortably.

'Your employer.' The tightening of his mouth informed her that her lack of manners had been noted. 'Who else?'

'No, of course he didn't.' The little flower, drooping slightly against the warmth of his body, was curiously affecting; she had an absurd longing to reach out, to touch the petals and incidentally to brush her fingers against his skin. Surely he *must* remember . . . 'Why should he?' Then she remembered exactly why Kulu would have been supposed to object to her outing with another man. 'He knows my feelings about these things, and . . . he has never tried to dictate my actions.'

'I see.' The smile he cast briefly towards her was not amused. 'So you go your own way.'

'We both do. Like most people these days. We aren't Victorian, after all.' Turning, she appeared to study closely the route they were travelling; in fact she was struggling for the control which was threatening to desert her completely. 'Where are we going?'

'Home.' Even as Rudi uttered the word in a sardonic kind of way they were turning through the high stone gates. 'It's the only place where we can be certain of peace to talk of all the things that must be discussed.'

They drew up at the front door. Arabella got out before he had time to come round and help, but a swift glance told her that the small flower had disappeared. She was uncertain whether it had dropped accidentally or whether he had removed it—until they were climbing the short flight of steps to the front door and she saw something drop from his fingers. A tiny, insignificant flower, crushed into a ball, fell on to the step in front of them, to be pulverised by a well-polished shoe.

'Now, Arabella.' They had settled into a smallish room overlooking a spacious flower garden, and the same silent woman whom she had met the previous evening brought a tray of coffee and then withdrew. 'You wanted to tell me something.' He was sitting at the far side of a large leather-topped desk, she in front of him, like the plaintive client of a condescending lawyer, she decided angrily.

'Yes. I'm sure you can imagine what I want to say.'

'I would rather you told me. I never find it advisable to allow my imagination to run away with me when business is being discussed.'

'I thought,' she spoke through clenched teeth, 'you were a writer, and therefore rather clever with your imagination.'

'We're talking about fact, not fiction.' A brief smile flitted over his face and disappeared. 'But let me make things easier for you, Arabella. Last night I asked you to marry me. I consider the night has given you time to reconsider your rather precipitate refusal.'

Irritated by his cold self-possessed way with words, she tried to glare, but his eyes were so intense it seemed simpler to transfer her attention to her fingers clamped round the strap of her handbag. 'Yes.' Showing nervousness could only be to her disadvantage. 'If your offer is still open, then I'd like to accept.'

It took him so long to reply that she felt cold little beads of sweat at the back of her neck, then at last she heard his voice, as low and slumbrous as ever it had been in the old days. 'Has something happened to persuade you to change your mind, Arabella? Or did you simply decide that . . . the prospect was not as unattractive as your reaction of last night indicated?'

'Of *course* something happened.' She would not have him thinking the decision was a voluntary one. The words came out with a little sob and she raised her head to show him how strong her animosity really was; she couldn't bear it if he got the impression that her attitude had softened. 'I rang home this morning and . . . didn't even recognise his voice.' Savagely she bit her lip, unable to continue.

'So you are worried, and . . .'

'Of course I'm worried! Wouldn't *you* be worried if your father was being threatened with prison?' In her distress she failed to notice a change in his expression, a sudden descent of bleakness, almost immediately wiped away as her eyes, blurred with tears, focused on him again. 'Please, Rudi,' now her tone was a shade more suppliant than it had been, 'will you help me?'

'*Natürlich*.' He had risen again to his feet, coming round the end of the desk to perch on the corner, one long leg swinging casually. 'Now, pour out some coffee. While we drink you will tell me as much as you can, then I shall speak with your father and arrange for funds to be placed at his disposal.'

'Thank you, Rudi.' She sniffed, perversely disappointed that he made no attempt to touch her. Surely in these circumstances it would have been natural for him to show a little tenderness, to put his arms about her and shield her from all the blows of Fate? Self-pity made her mouth tremble again, but she reached for the pot and filled two cups, passing one to him, watching him stir briefly, then drink.

'Here's to us, Arabella. *Prosit*. I'm sure our marriage will be very successful. Now . . .' There was a significance in the pause which escaped her just then; she was too conscious that he had moved away from her, emotionally as well as physically, returning to the far side of the desk, pulling a pad towards him, making a few notes which he frowned over. 'We must decide on a date. It would be best to have that out of the way before I speak to your father.'

'A date?' That she was utterly bewildered her expression showed very clearly.

'A date for our wedding, Arabella,' he explained patiently.

'For our wedding? But . . . surely there's no rush for that?'

'Didn't you tell me, *Liebling*, that your father had to have this sum of money within a few days?'

'Yes, but . . .'

'And I said I would clear those outstanding debts if you would agree to marry me.'

She stared, unable to absorb totally what he was saying. Then Rudi continued. 'These must coincide, Arabella. In arranged marriages such as ours . . .'

'Arranged marriages?' Racked indignation made her voice strident. 'What on earth do you mean?'

'Calm down.' He frowned impatiently. 'The arranged marriage is still fairly common in Europe, and from what I've observed it's at least as successful as the conventional kind. And they almost always involve some kind of business arrangement; it's quite usual. What I'm saying is that they invariably coincide as far as time is concerned. So . . . as your father's problems are rather urgent, then I'm afraid I'll have to insist that the wedding plans are put into operation right away. In fact'—hurriedly he consulted the engagement diary lying open on his desk—'I would suggest next Wednesday. If you would agree to that, I shall arrange for the funds to be released then, and . . .'

'It sounds extremely cold-blooded.' Her lips could barely form the words.

'Not really.' He spared her a brief smile. 'In fact, when you look as charming as you do this morning, my dear'—his diary had reclaimed his attention—'cold-blooded . . . is the . . . last thing I feel. Yes,' he looked up again, seeming oblivious of the grimness in her expression, 'I think Wednesday would be all right. I suggest we travel down to Bavaria and marry there. Perhaps your father would care to come out and give you away. You would like that, and maybe you could persuade one of your friends to travel down with us, to keep you company till after the ceremony.'

'If that's what you have planned,' she agreed coldly.

'I think it would be best. Now,' he pushed the telephone across the table, 'if you would like to get your father. Perhaps our news would be best coming from you. Then he and I can get down to business when he has had time to recover from the shock.'

Arabella's fingers shook as she found the digits, but at last she succeeded, and to her relief he sounded much more like the real Gordon Smythe than he had earlier. Afterwards she thought it was the most difficult thing she had ever done in her life, telling her father she was about to make a hurried marriage to a man whom he had never heard of. But if it was a shock he concealed it admirably, possibly because his mind was wholly preoccupied with his business worries.

'Darling, are you sure? It does seem rather hurried.'

'I know, Daddy.' Too conscious of Rudi's dark scrutiny, she swung round so that her face was at least partly hidden. 'And of course we're sure. And please'—here for the first time her voice trembled,

forcing her to pause for a few seconds—'please
come out to Bavaria and give me away. It would
quite spoil my wedding if you were unable to be
there.'

'Wednesday?' Still he sounded abstracted, and
Arabella wondered if perhaps his accountant was
hovering somewhere in the background. 'Well, I'm
not sure. Bavaria, you say? Is there no way you
could be married in England? It would be so much
more convenient—all your friends . . .'

'But we shan't be having a huge wedding, Daddy.
Neither of us wants that, but you must say you'll
come. Look, I'll put Rudi on; he'll be able to
persuade you. 'Bye.' And without waiting for a
reply she thrust the receiver across the desk, felt it
taken from her fingers.

While Rudi talked she got up, crossed to the
window and stared out, seeing nothing of the
carefully tended lawn with the contrived gaps
leading down to the Grünewalder See, aware only
of the necessity of gaining some control before she
was forced to speak again with Rudi. She couldn't
bear it, being simply bartered like this. And just to
repay some foolish business deals made by her
father. It wasn't fair. And yet—she shivered—if
anyone had told her last week that soon she'd be
marrying Rudi Schlegel she would have been filled
with the most tremulous reactions, the most
indescribable joy, would have imagined the passion
which had existed between them had been waiting,
ready to be rekindled into a blazing furnace. Instead
of which she was being forced into marriage with a
total stranger. Collateral for a large loan.

'Arabella.' Rudi's voice made her turn from the
window, her whole manner betraying profound
reluctance, to find him holding the receiver out to
her. 'You would like to have a last word with your
father?' Without speaking she shook her head, and
slowly he took the telephone back to his ear and

they stared at each other while he concluded the conversation.

'*Ja. Ja.* I understand. Well, goodbye, Gordon.' The familiarity was amazing. 'We shall hope to see you next Wednesday. She would be so disappointed if . . . *Ja*,' a short laugh. '*Auf wiederhören.*' And the dark red receiver was replaced in its cradle.

'I am sure he will come.' He crossed towards her, his feet silent on the thick carpet, his eyes taking in every detail of her appearance and doubtless missing nothing of her distress. 'That is what you want, *nicht wahr*?'

Arabella nodded, biting her lip feverishly. What did anyone know or care about what *she* wanted? But every word he spoke seemed to make her more fraught, more inarticulate.

'Well'—his sigh was so faint she probably imagined it—'perhaps you would like to spend the afternoon in town, shopping. I shall give you money in case you see anything you want to buy.'

'I have enough money.' Dark, guilty colour stained her cheek, but she had no intention of taking from him until they were married, until the price was paid. In the meantime, she was still her own person.

'Very well.' He glanced at his watch. 'I was going to suggest we have an early lunch together. Unfortunately I have much to do this afternoon, but I can put Ernst at your disposal. Oh, and by the way, I would prefer you to pick up your things and move into a hotel until we leave for Bavaria.'

'Very well.' Her mutinous look was meant to show him she understood perfectly that he was putting a sold sign on the goods he was purchasing on Wednesday and that he had no liking for the idea that they might be tried out by someone else in the meantime. But she refused to blush, looking back at him with quite brazen indifference and deciding against telling him that Kulu was leaving for home this evening.

'You have a friend you would like to remain with you?'

'Yes, there's Caroline. The girl you met last night. But I'm sure she'll have to go home; she has a charity show on Sunday. I might be able to persuade her to come out again for . . . for Wednesday.'

'Good. I would like you to have some friends round you.'

'In that case, there are several others I would like to invite.' There was no reason why she should be a complete doormat, and if she had been marrying in different circumstances she would have had the freedom to compile her own guest list.

'By all means.' He was beginning to sound like the conventional tender fiancé: indulgent, loving. 'Ask whom you like, Arabella. All your friends will be welcome.'

'There aren't so many who'll be free to come over at such short notice, but Caroline and I have been friends for several years. And there's Kulu, of course, and maybe . . .'

'Kulu?' If he had been suffering from a mood of tender indulgence a moment before that name was enough to dispel it utterly. His head jerked up to look fiercely at her, eyes blazed with what might have been simple jealousy but was much more likely to be angry pride. Whatever, she was in no mood to succumb cravenly.

'Yes.' Idly Arabella walked to the window and looked out, one hand outstretched against the rich material of the curtains. 'I've worked for him for a long time, remember. He's been kind to me in any number of ways and . . .'

'I'd rather you didn't invite him to our wedding,' Rudi said.

'But why not?' She gave a mocking little laugh. 'You said all my friends would be welcome and . . .'

'All your friends. Except that one.'

'And I suppose'—filled with sudden almost uncontrollable anger she whirled round to look at him—'I'll have a veto on whichever of your friends displease me.' Her chest heaved with suppressed rage.

'If you feel strongly enough about it. But I can imagine no circumstances in which that is likely to happen, so let's leave the matter there, shall we? There's no point in quarrelling.'

'And that . . . is your last word?' Sparks flew from her eyes.

'On that subject, but . . .'

'In that case,' with a sudden change of direction she spoke with calm sweetness, 'I'll just have those two guests. My father and Caroline. I'm not prepared to risk any other names which might for some reason meet with your disapproval.'

'As you please.' Realising that he was struggling to control his irritation, Arabella felt a small throb of satisfaction, turning away to hide her smile. When he understood just how much he had misunderstood her relationship with Kulu then he was bound to beg her forgiveness. Besides, she was very sure that Kulu would be unavailable next week; he had plans for flying to New York and she would be safe to give him a private invitation in the certainty of his refusal.

During lunch, served again by the housekeeper but now rendered garrulous by the glass of champagne Rudi insisted she drink, Arabella heard the name of Frau von Schlegel come up several times. At first she assumed the references were to the person she was soon to become, but Rudi's reply to her enquiry caused her fork to drop with a clatter on to her plate.

'My mother lives in Bavaria. That is why I have chosen the situation for our marriage.'

'Oh?' She waited for him to say more, to offer some further information, and when it became clear that he would not, she raised a fork with a few morsels of food. It was impossible for her to pretend that this sudden materialisation of a close relative hadn't shocked her, and she tried to dredge up from the past the little he had told her about his family. His parents had lived in the east, and since he hadn't mentioned them she had assumed that they would be there still.

'So . . .' He threw down his napkin and came round to refill her glass. 'You will be able to amuse yourself this afternoon, Arabella?'

'Of course.' Her tone assured him she preferred things that way. 'Perfectly.' Refusing to look at him, she took the glass to her lips again. 'In fact, Caroline said she was going window-shopping; I might as well join her.'

'Then, if you tell Ernst where you wish to go . . . And arrange a time for him to collect you. I shall find a suitable hotel and come to pick you up this evening. We shall do something special to celebrate.'

Swiftly she looked across the table, trying to decide whether or not she had heard a sardonic note in his voice, but his face was impassive as ever. Celebrate? Briefly she considered the word, then dismissed it. Certainly no one looking in on them now would have the faintest idea that they were planning their wedding.

The opening of the door was signalled by a rattle of crockery, Arabella allowed herself a grim little smile as she suspected Frau Fischer of tactfully allowing them a little time to spring apart from a passionate embrace. The woman even looked faintly disappointed to see them sitting so staidly opposite each other, but she smiled fatuously at the girl as she placed a dish of strawberries and two plates in

front of her, then left the coffee things on the
sideboard, explaining to Rudi that this arrangement
meant they would not be disturbed again. Arabella
felt warmth in her cheeks, and glanced quickly
towards him, then dropped her long lashes as she
encountered an amused expression.

'I'll give you this.' He took a plastic card from his
pocket and pushed it across the table. 'In case you
see anything you want to buy; I'll ring the bank and
clear it for you.' He leaned his elbows on the table,
rested his chin on linked fingers. 'There are bound
to be things you want, Arabella—things as obvious
as a wedding dress,' his voice was mellow, indulgent
as any doting fiancé, 'and don't tell me that you
brought enough money with you for things like
that, for I simply shan't believe you.'

How humiliating, to be reminded that she was
marrying him because he was rich; she didn't think
she could *bear* to be any more in his debt. 'I have
no need to buy a dress . . . I have one that will do
perfectly well.' The lie came easily and she raised
her head to glare defiance should he try to persuade
her. And suddenly, unable to bear the expression
on his face, she stared down at her plate again.

'If you say so.' Considering how insulting she had
made her tone, his was mild. Perhaps, the thought
occurred to her much later, he was remembering
his own reaction in a similar situation, understanding
how she felt. 'But remember, Arabella, that once
we are married you will find it impossible to thwart
me in this.' He pushed back his chair and came to
stand behind hers, then he bent down so that she
was aware of the faint rasp of his cheek against
hers. 'One of the great rewards of being wealthy is
being able to indulge all the wishes of those . . .
those closest to you.' Arabella had the almost
overwhelming longing to turn her face; a mere inch
would bring their mouths into contact, and . . . She
waited too long and he moved across to the

sideboard to pour out coffee. 'And that is the one thing I am determined you won't deny me. Then . . . I shall pick you up about seven this evening. Oh, and wear a long dress. It's going to be that kind of occasion.'

'I can't believe it, Bella!' The two girls were sitting in one of the glass-fronted coffee houses on the Kurfürstendamm. Caroline was cradling her cup in her hands and her eyes were as wide as saucers. 'Marrying him!' She frowned her perplexity. 'Even I wouldn't dream of marrying a man I met yesterday.'

'But I told you, I knew Rudi quite well five years ago.'

'Yes, I know you said that, but . . . you've never seen him since. Not till the other night.'

'I suppose it sounds crazy.' Even to her own ears she was unconvincing. 'But we were madly in love then.'

'So madly in love that you didn't even write to each other in all the five years?'

Arabella shrugged, trying to appear blasé. 'I suppose it's bound to seem like that to you, Caroline. But remember, I was very young, and it would have been madness to marry.' Here she was, contradicting all the fiercely held passions of her youth. 'Now we're both old enough to know our own minds. *And*,' she gave a light little laugh, 'old enough to please ourselves.'

'What about your father? I know mine would go mad if I did anything like this. He'd come out and drag me home by the hair!'

'I'm sure he'd do no such thing. At least, he might start out with that intention, but half an hour after he'd arrived you'd have him eating out of your hand and trying to bring forward the wedding date a day or two.'

Caroline giggled, spluttered into her cup and

choked. 'You're right, I'm afraid.' She wiped her mouth with a tissue, then held out her cup for a refill. 'Mum says I've been twisting him round my little finger since I was six months old. Besides,' she went on reflectively, 'he would probably be intrigued to have a bestselling author in the family. What's the book about—do tell me.'

'I . . . I don't know.' What a humiliating admission to have to make. 'I haven't had a chance to read it.'

'What?' Of course Caroline couldn't resist such an opportunity. 'You don't mean you're going to marry the man and you haven't taken the trouble to read his book yet? It is, after all,' she grew matronly and confidential, 'the thing that's going to keep you in comfort for the rest of your lives.'

'I haven't had much time, have I?' Arabella had no intention of even pretending to be frank with Caroline. 'We haven't had a minute since we arrived in Berlin, but I'm going to buy a copy before I go back to pick up my case.'

'Well, you can buy one for me too. Help keep up the royalties. If I'm to come to Munich to be your bridesmaid on Wednesday, I'd better know something about the man you're going to marry.'

'Oh, Caro!' Surprisingly Arabella felt the sting of tears behind her eyes, and realised for the first time just how lonely and isolated she had been feeling. 'Thank you.' Reaching out across the table she squeezed her friend's hand.

'Don't thank me.' As she pushed back her chair Caroline grinned. 'Just line up a dishy best man. I don't want to spoil things by being wildly jealous.'

'I'll try.' Arabella made an attempt to smile, but couldn't help realising just how little she knew about Rudi. Did he even have a friend who would be willing to act as his best man? It seemed a chillingly unlikely thought.

She was waiting, trying to subdue her anxiety, for

Rudi to come to the hotel and pick her up. The
hotel where she was temporarily lodged was
completely unknown to her, but it was the most
elegantly luxurious she had ever seen. Tucked away
from the city bustle in its own spacious grounds, it
was more like a prestigious embassy than a hotel,
and inside all was silence except for the occasional
swish of lift doors or the muffled ringing of a
telephone. Her room had silk-lined walls the colour
of fading pink roses, and the curtains hanging at
the tall windows were in a deeper shade with swags
of gold cord. The room was large enough to hold a
comfortable sofa and two easy chairs as well as the
two beds, and the adjoining bathroom was lined
with mirrors which gave her little chance to avoid
the evidence of her own nervousness.

A bell rang startlingly, and for a moment she was
unable to find the source until she remembered the
telephone in the tiny hall. She hurried to pick it up.

'*Fraülein*.' She heard the impeccable well-modula-
ted voice of the beautiful blonde in reception. 'Herr
von Schlegel has arrived and is on his way up.'

'Thank you. *Danke schön*.' And the instrument
fell from her fingers.

What would he think? As if she hadn't seen
enough of it, she stared at her reflection again.
Immaculately groomed. Beautiful. She was so used
to her own appearance that she could be totally
dispassionate about it, quite devoid of vanity, seeing
it simply as a tool of her trade. But she was looking
attractive. Since her return from shopping she had
washed her hair, brushing it out in the simple style
she preferred, making a soft frame for her face.
Eyes, a bit more defensive than usual but with
eyebrows well marked, lashes emphasised . . .
mouth, this soft pink with just a hint of brown
suited her colouring.

A knock at the door brought her heart into a
wild reaction, and she whirled away before she

could see she deserved some congratulation for the
ice-blue satin she was wearing. Utterly plain but for
some skilful draping to where it knotted on one
shoulder, it drew attention to her delicately slender
figure, and it was only when she moved that the slit
from ankle to thigh was revealed.

Rudi didn't speak at once, simply stood there, his
dark eyes noting every detail even to the dangling
crystal earrings which she had inherited from her
great-grandmother. And while he was studying her
she was looking at him with an intensity that had a
hint of fever, forgetting everything that had marred
the last few days, oblivious of everything except
that he had come, the man she had loved for so
long. At *last* he had come for her.

'Arabella.' As she stepped backwards he came
into the hall, and behind her she felt the door hit
the small of her back, blocking their passage into
the bedroom, almost forcing them into the close
proximity she would rather have avoided. Vaguely
she realised he had pushed the outer door, that the
cellophane box of flowers he carried had been
tossed on to a side table.

'Arabella.' He spoke her name again, but gently
lingering over it, the throb in his voice that spoke
of remembered sorrow bringing a painful ache to
her chest. His hand came out, took hers and raised
it to his lips while his eyes continued to hold hers.

The formal contact, the feel of his mouth against
her skin on even such an insensitive part as the
back of her hand, caused her to jerk, to shiver a
little in fear of her own reaction, especially when
she saw his eyes absorb each detail of her
appearance. Down, then a lazy drift upwards,
intent, absorbing. 'You look,' his voice rubbed
down her spine, and she was barely conscious that
his fingers still held hers, that he was persuading her
body towards his, 'quite stunning, *mein Schätzchen*.'
That word, with all its tender implications, melted

any resistance her logical being was struggling to retain, so when he pulled her masterfully into his arms, when his mouth came down on hers, she felt herself melt against him, willing all the unhappy years to whirl away, out of memory.

Had he always been this expert? His mouth left hers, traced a dizzying path over closed eyelids, along the curve of her cheekbones, down to the corner of her lips which parted willingly to his delicate, unhurried exploration.

She heard her voice murmuring a tiny protest as his lips moved to the arch of her throat and lower. Her heart was hammering wildly and her searching fingers on his chest felt an echo of that excitement, and then, as all the restraint began to slip away, when the sweet fire burned in her veins, she was held away from him. 'Perhaps, *Liebling*, we'd better go. Or we shall be late.'

CHAPTER SIX

ARABELLA refused to try to subdue the tide of anger
that washed over her as she sat stiffly by his side.
Even the timeless beauty of the music could not
soften her, could not reconcile her to the fact that
he had brought her to the Opern Haus to listen to
that woman. On this evening, the evening which he
had assured her was to be a celebration, she was
forced to sit and smile, to feign pleasure when the
only emotion she could register was overwhelming
jealousy. To know that Klara Steyr had been
expecting them, or at least him, that when she
reached the tenderest part of some beguiling love
song she would turn, directing her words to this
side box just above the stage, her arms, so rounded
and creamy as they emerged from black velvet,
held up beseechingly! Didn't he care what people
thought? Didn't he care if she put the worst possible
construction on their relationship?

To be honest, Rudi showed very little reaction
to Klara's blandishments; he sat through the
programme, relaxed but intent, showing his appreci-
ation only at the end of each piece when the
whole auditorium exploded enthusiastically. Quite
deliberately Arabella restrained her own response,
although there were times, when Klara was not on
the stage, when she had been in danger of allowing
the melodies to seduce her.

There had been that selection of operetta music
by Léhar, so emotional and romantic that she had
longed to dance. If she half closed her eyes, allowed

herself to sway in time to the music, she could imagine being swept round a ballroom in Rudi's arms. Then accidentally she had looked up and found that he was watching her, and for a moment the expression in his eyes had made her heart falter, then race in wild excitement. She ran the tip of her tongue over suddenly dry lips, imagined that his hand was reaching out to hers and . . .

Klara's voice, rich and dominant, soared about them, stifling, disruptive, and Arabella returned her attention to the stage—then spent the next ten minutes whipping up her indignation against him.

How dared he drag her along here when she had imagined they would spend the evening alone together, somewhere they could perhaps dance? Why else could she have imagined she would be required to wear a long dress? The thought of the theatre hadn't even crossed her mind.

'You enjoyed the programme?' Now it was over, and the smart audience was beginning to leave. Rudi was standing waiting while she picked up her shawl and draped it over her arm.

'Yes, enormously,' she lied, refusing to look at him.

'I'm glad.' He took her wrap to place it about her shoulders. 'And now we have been invited backstage to have a drink with Klara.'

'Oh.' Her tone was deliberately non-committal. Why let him know that she found his friendship with another woman hurtful? Much better to pretend indifference to his actions. After all, she fanned her bitterness, it *was* only their engagement party, so why should she have imagined she would be alone with him?

She was silent as she followed him along corridors, through a door marked private and into the back of the theatre, and Rudi himself seemed to have little enough to say until they reached an open door

through which came the babble of voices and
laughter.

'Klara.' Even so self-contained a man as Rudi
Schlegel could occasionally give the impression of
being slightly nervous. 'I think you have met
Arabella Smythe.'

'No, I am sure not.' Klara, following his lead,
spoke in English, in which she seemed to be as easy
as in her own tongue. She smiled, but there was a
hint of steel in the brilliant blue eyes which flicked
comprehensively over the other girl before returning
more warmly to the man. 'Otherwise I should
remember.'

'Well, perhaps not.' Rudi's response was relaxed.
'But you were both at Frau Steffan's.'

'I see.' Klara was thoughtful. 'Strange that no
one introduced us.'

'But I didn't meet everyone.' Arabella was in no
mood to be patronised. 'Most of the time I was
supposed to be working, after all.'

'Working?' Klara frowned in concentration, and
Arabella almost laughed. It was obvious that the
woman was trying to place her among the small
army of waitresses who had kept things going.

'I work for Kulu. I'm one of his models.'

'Oh, of course.' But something about the expression on the older woman's face told Arabella that
not for a moment had she been forgotten.

'And Arabella and I have some news for you,
Klara.' Rudi interrupted firmly, as if he had
something to get off his chest and would be happy
only when he had done so. Arabella, watching
Klara who now was concentrating on Rudi, saw a
strange expression on her face, as if suddenly
understanding exactly what that news might be.
Understanding and being shocked by it. 'We are to
be married next week.' His fingers reached out,
found Arabella's and pulled her to his side. 'And I

hope, we both hope, that you will come down to Bayern and join us for the ceremony.'

Shock filmed her eyes for just a split second, the jaw dropped momentarily, the mouth trembled until she caught it with small white teeth. Then with brilliant self-control the expression was transformed into surprise. And delight. Oh yes, there were no half measures about her reaction; Klara Steyr, gifted actress and singer, was quite bowled over by the news of her friend's wedding, and the embraces she pressed on both of them could hardly be distinguished from the real thing.

It was only when she faced Arabella squarely, when she was totally assured that Rudi could not see, that her true message was unswervingly transmitted. You need not imagine for one minute, the cold blue eyes glittered wildly, that this makes any difference. What we have been to each other we shall still, we shall always be. And no little English model, whether he chooses to marry her or not, will make the slightest difference to our relationship.

Just for a moment she stared at Arabella, then with a complete change of mood she swung round, conveying the happy news to the others in the room with every indication of extreme pleasure. So convincing was she that Arabella might have thought she was imagining the other reaction, but she happened to intercept exchanged glances between two of the women present, eyebrows raised almost into their elaborate hairdos, mouths pulled down in silent amused speculation. Nothing could have told Arabella more clearly that all their acquaintances were aware of the type of friendship which existed between Rudi and Klara, and that they would watch developments with interest.

Before she understood what was happening she found herself with a glass of sparkling wine in her hand; there were congratulations and good wishes, most of them apparently genuine, and a number of ponderous compliments to herself from several of the men present. But when her glass was refilled, suddenly she felt she must escape from the synthetic air of celebration, and she withdrew unobtrusively to the powder room she had noticed when she was coming in.

Waves of nausea assaulted her, but soon passed after she had splashed some cold water over her face, and she was repairing her make-up in a tiny alcove when she heard the door behind her open and recognised the voices of the two young women whom she had noticed earlier.

At first she paid no attention to what they were saying, but at last she heard one word being laughingly repeated and was forced to listen more closely. The hand wielding the lip brush paused as she concentrated on the conversation. But how much better if she hadn't!

When the door banged closed behind the two unseen speakers she was still sitting, unmoving, staring at her reflection, bruised and vulnerable. If only I hadn't heard them. Or if I had let them know I was sitting here, listening to a conversation they had thought was private.

Then I would not be tormented by the innuendo, the suggestions—nothing more definite—that a torrid and long-lasting romance had been interrupted. Or possibly not interrupted—she thought she caught that giggling implication correctly—by Rudi Schlegel meeting up with the girl.

That was one of the puzzling aspects of what she had overheard, the faintly emphatic repetition of *das Mädchen*, the girl, as if she were one in particular. Of course she could easily have misunderstood or misheard or something, but somehow she was convinced that the general message was clear enough. Everyone was standing back, watching and waiting, anxious to see just how long it would be before the old relationship would be resumed. That is, if he gave her up in the first place. He would not be the first man, so one of the young Berlin matrons told her friend with satisfaction, to keep a lover happy while breaking in a new wife. And of course, she babbled on happily as further possibilities sprang up in her fertile imagination: we all know how mad he is for the opera. I quite firmly believe that is half Klara's attraction for him.

Finally Arabella forced herself to get up. The last thing she wanted was for Rudi to send someone into the powder room in search of her. She drew a shuddering sigh and faced her reflection, thinking how wan and tired she looked. Not that she cared much after what she had heard. At least . . . she was almost certain . . . Possibly she could have been wrong; her ear still wasn't attuned to the language as it had once been. Suppose she had allowed them to express all those ideas she was trying to hide from herself. . . Oh no, she was becoming too fraught, unable to distinguish fact from fiction. She knew what she had heard.

'Arabella.' Rudi was waiting, and at once stepped towards her, eyes full of concern, as she would have seen if she had taken the trouble to do more than glance at him. 'Are you all right, *Liebling*?' His voice was low, tender.

'Of course. It's just been rather a busy day.' Her tone was sharp.

'Perhaps . . . There has been a suggestion that we all go on to a nightclub. Some people are intent on celebrating,' she was uncertain whether the curled lip was meant to indicate amusement or disdain, 'but of course if you are tired and would prefer to go back to the hotel . . .'

Sensing that was his preference, Arabella was at once suffused by panic. The very last thing she could cope with right now, after what she had just learned, was Rudi von Schlegel's undivided attention. If she was sufficiently tempted then her indignation might just boil over and she would tell him exactly what she thought of him. And she was hardly in a position to do that. After the wedding would be time enough. So she smiled brilliantly round the company, tried to ignore the way Rudi's eyebrows were drawn together in a frown, and said, 'What a wonderful idea, I can't think of anything I'd like more.'

But before she had been in Kaliban's for more than ten minutes she was wondering what on earth had possessed her to prolong the evening. Her ears ached with the volume of the jazz trumpets and, arriving so late and in such a large party, they had had to be content with a table fairly close to the stage. Complementing the trumpets, the drummers were a fairly busy pair, and Arabella felt their pulse continue even when they stopped playing.

Apart from that, she would hardly have been surprised to see Sally Bowles herself lounging in one of the doorways leading to the back stage. It was all done up very much in the twenties mode, girls with flour-white faces, hectically rouged, kohl-eyed, sang raucous and, judging from the guffaws, slightly suggestive songs while they draped themselves round unresponsive, deliberately brutal-looking men. It was not the kind of show she enjoyed, and her effort to conceal her distaste resulted perversely in an appearance of exaggerated pleasure of which she was certain Rudi would disapprove.

But after a time the music grew less strident, and a tiny circle was cleared so that the customers could dance. Arabella found herself on the floor, being held very close to one of the group, a stoutish man called Walther who had been giving her slumbrous looks for the better part of the evening. Walther was the only one who spoke barely any English and he contented himself with breathing heavily, significantly into her ear, his short fair beard tickling her cheek while he held her firmly against his protuberant stomach.

The floor was so small and overcrowded that dancing was almost impossible, a circling shuffle the best that could be achieved, and the interval was an excuse for a little discreet, or not so discreet, lovemaking. Rudi, she saw, was dancing with Klara—who else?—and as they passed close Arabella looked straight through him, hoping that he would get the message that she was not having the time of her life.

Almost at once, she found that there had been a switch of partners, all achieved in the most good-humoured way possible, of course, but she was fairly certain from their facial expressions that neither Klara nor Walther approved.

'I'm sorry,' Rudi looked down searchingly into her face, 'you are finding it all a terrible bore.' His arm tightened marginally about her waist, and his thumb moved experimentally against her palm.

'No, not really,' Such intimate contact made her voice shake, her fingers throbbed as the blood in her veins began to race wildly, and in gathering panic she wondered if she preferred Walther after all. Certainly there was a degree of safety in the portly figure, while being held like this, against the taut strength of the man who was Rudi Schlegel, was fraught with temptation and danger. Sexual desire swelled as she looked up into Rudi's face, her eyes wide and helpless, and the expression she saw did little to damp down her feelings. He bent his head close to hers, she felt the warmth of their breath mingling and . . . Klara came close and spoke in rapid German, words which deliberately excluded Arabella, quite spoiling her fragile tentative mood and certainly the moment.

'Let's go.' Rudi spoke roughly as he seized her

arm, pulling her away from the throng of bodies, back to the table where he made polite but firm excuses for their premature flight.

But before they were able to depart from the nightclub, Klara, Walther following behind her, intercepted them in the foyer with loud protestations that they must not go so early.

'We are going.' Something about Rudi's tone suggested that he was rapidly losing patience, and his reply, in German, was short and definite.

'Oh, very well.' Klara pouted in disappointment. 'But you are usually the one who wants to keep going when the rest of us flake out, Rudi. I hope that marriage will not change you so much.' The private glance she sent to Arabella was brilliant with malice. 'We all rather like you as you are.' And her hand went up to remove a few imaginary specks from Rudi's jacket, much in the same way as a wife might have done. 'Well goodnight, *Liebling*.' She leaned towards him to accept his kiss. 'And you, Arabella.' Their cheeks almost touched; Arabella felt herself smiling insincerely, and her own voice was murmuring something about next week's wedding and her hope that she would be one of the guests.

'Of course, I shall let you have the details, Klara. Goodnight. Goodnight, Walther.' His hand was on her arm and she allowed herself to be manipulated towards the door, as he would, she presumed, expect to control her for the rest of their lives together.

The journey back to the hotel was as silent as the outward one had been, giving Arabella time to brood and meditate on all that had happened during the evening. Inevitably her mind kept returning to what she had overheard in the powder room, and all the implications seemed to magnify and multiply the more she considered them.

If she had the courage, she should face him with

the knowledge—face him and demand that his
relationship with Klara should end immediately and
for ever. But suppose his answer to that was to
cancel the wedding and in a single gesture, cut off
her father's lifeline? No, she must show discretion,
wait at least until they were married and her father
safe; then and only then would be the time to make
demands on him, tell him exactly what she was
prepared to put up with in their marriage. There
had been a moment earlier in the evening when it
had been on the tip of her tongue to reject Klara
Steyr as a guest at their wedding in the same way as
he had refused Kulu an invitation. She could hardly
imagine what had stopped her, except perhaps the
suspicion—more than that, the certainty—that he
would have brushed aside her wishes as trivial and
petty. And she didn't think she could bear such
accusations right now. She shivered as if the warm
summer evening had turned suddenly chilly and
looked up in surprise as the car slid to a halt
outside her hotel.

'Will . . . will you come up?' Rudi was holding
open the car door for her.

'I think it best not to, don't you.' When she
didn't reply he took her fingertips, raised them to
his lips, brushed them against his mouth, apparently
oblivious of the shiver that racked her again, nor
noticing the wide eyes, dark and shadowy in the
moonlight, nervous and bewildered. 'Goodnight,
Arabella.' His voice held all the gentle cadences
which had once thrilled her; there was tenderness
as well as a flash of something more urgent in his
coal-black gaze. 'Arabella.' Now his tone was so
forceful, infinitely less controlled, and his hand
brushed aside her wrap, sliding swiftly up the length
of her arm to the shoulder where her dress was so
casually knotted. '*Mein Schätzchen.*' Had he spoken
the words, or were they simply the longing of her
fevered imagination? His head inclined towards her,

she felt the warmth of his breath against her cheek, his mouth reached the corner of hers before she, with a nervously indrawn breath, pulled back. Loud in her ears was the clamour of pulses, her own and his, then, eyes still gleaming with urgency among the shadowed planes of his face, he spoke. 'Goodnight, Arabella.' Now the kiss he dropped on her cheek was chaste and unemotional. '*Bis Morgen.*' And he turned away.

Until she reached the comfort of her bedroom she was able to control the tears that were aching in her breast. Damn him! Damn him! As she threw herself on to the silk cover they came washing down her cheeks in a torrent until at last, the violence of her feelings abated, calm returned, and she rolled over, reaching out for the rose-coloured tissues beside the table lamp. And when she had wiped her face she lay on her back for a long time, looking at the plaster ornamentation on the ceiling. How stupid of her to give way to such absurd emotion; it had been the last thing in her mind while they had been in the car when she had been so angry with him.

But then he had taken advantage of her, had shown tenderness, had called her his love when all the time they were marrying for convenience. Well, he couldn't have it both ways. If he wanted a wife then he must forgo Klara Steyr, mistress or not and if he refused . . . Her mind blanked off that possibility, for she really had no confidence in her own reaction. Once she and Rudi were lovers, then she doubted that she would ever have the strength to leave him. That brief episode downstairs had shown her as much, when his fingers had moved up her arm, like the most blatant caress from any other man.

Chemical reaction, that was all it was, the kind to which men were subject when in the company of any reasonably attractive woman. It didn't *mean* anything.

Abruptly she swung her feet on to the floor, at the same time reaching for another tissue to obliterate the residue of her distress. And as she fumbled, she knocked something from the bedside table on to the floor, something which fell with a thud on to the deep soft carpet. As she bent to pick it up, Rudi's eyes looked directly at her from the cover of his book. He had been photographed at a desk, chin supported by one hand while he looked pensively into the mid-distance.

An aspect of the photograph caught at her, held her so that her breathing was constricted, she was unaware that one of her fingers slipped over his features in a caressing movement. She was equally unconscious of having opened the book till she began to read the biographical details in the inside cover.

'Rudi von Schlegel,' she was informed, 'is one of the most remarkable writers to emerge from Germany in the latter part of the twentieth century. Unknown except to an inner circle of cognoscenti, he has stunned the literary world with his first major work of fiction. No one who reads *An Old Affair* can fail to be moved by the sensuous beauty of the writing when it deals with the central doomed love story, nor can fail to wonder that from the same pen came the savagely sardonic sideways swipes at the idiocies of political theorists and their baleful influence on the lives of people. Rudi von Schlegel has written a book no one will be able to forget, a powerful warning to governments and governed alike and a joyful exaltation of the human spirit.'

Arabella felt the book slip from her fingers on to the bed. She hadn't known, hadn't understood just how important a figure she was about to marry. In spite of the piles of books which she had seen in

the bookshop where she had picked up the English
versions, one in paperback for Caroline who would
almost certainly never get round to reading it,
hardback for herself, she had felt as she handed
over an enormous sum in Deutschmarks that it was
the least she could do. And they were selling like
hot cakes; she had been forced to join a jostling
crowd round the cash desk—the Berliners didn't
believe in queueing like normal people.

Hurriedly Arabella got into bed and began to
read, but she found the first few pages complex and
slow, about a family at the beginning of the century
who lived in a remote German province on the
Baltic. How disappointing. From the blurb she had
imagined that in some strange way it would give her
a clue as to what Rudi had been doing in the
intervening years. She yawned, closing the book
with a feeling of anti-climax. Some time later, when
she was less exhausted, she would read it. But right
now . . . She reached for the light switch and put
her head comfortably on the pillow. . .

The swish of heavy curtains being pulled back
wakened her, and a maid stood waiting with a tray
while she struggled into a sitting position.

'*Fräulein. Guten Tag.*' The girl smiled.

'*Guten Tag.*' Swiftly Arabella stifled a yawn. 'I
didn't order breakfast; I never eat it . . .'

'Oh, Herr von Schlegel ordered it for you last
night.' She placed the tray on Arabella's knees,
murmuring '*Guten Appetit*,' before closing the door
behind her.

The first thing Arabella saw was the single red
rose laid on top of the immaculately laundered
linen napkin. Thoughtfully she took it to her nose
and sniffed, enjoying the faint perfume. Had it
come from Rudi? she wondered. Once, long ago,
she had waited at a roadside stall while he went and
spoke to the woman and then returned with a single
long-stemmed rose which he offered with that

slightly formal gesture which was such a feature of life in Berlin—not quite a bow, not quite a click of the heels, but with much to suggest both. Terribly gallant, disturbingly romantic. She had taken it, shy as much for the expression in his eyes as for the method of presentation. But delighted with both.

Of course, she thought as she lay back on the piled pillows drinking the strong, scalding coffee, eating a crisp roll with butter, giving a single flower was so much a custom of the country; she couldn't be certain that it didn't happen with every single visitor in such a splendid hotel. So of course she would say nothing. How intolerable to thank him and be returned a blank uncomprehending stare.

By the time she had showered and dressed, Arabella was feeling much more relaxed than she had been the previous evening. Then her nerves had been stretched and she had most likely over-reacted to what had happened. Many of the glances which she had seen exchanged between Klara and Rudi could have been the result of an over-active imagination, and even the conversation was only what might have been expected. Rudi was bound to have had his share of women-friends; few men of his age would be celibate, and it was up to her to ensure that after they were married, he would have no interest in his old affair—she smiled at her choice of words—with Klara Steyr.

Much of her self-confidence was restored, and her reflection completed the job. A good night's sleep was the most marvellous beauty aid, and in spite of everything she had slept well. The coffee and rolls had done the rest. On impulse she took the rose from the tray, broke off the stem and slipped it into the top pocket of her jacket, where it stood out against the white handkerchief. It wasn't absolutely what she would have chosen to go with pink wool, but at least it might elicit some remark which would tell her if he had sent it. It might even let him know that she, too, had a share of sentiment . . . Humming to herself, she picked up the telephone when it began to ring, a throb of something remarkably like pleasure stirring at the certainty that Rudi had arrived.

'Daddy!' She was delighted when she heard his voice, but could not quite subdue a feeling of apprehension engendered by such an early call. 'Is there . . .'

'No, there's nothing wrong if that's what you're going to ask.' He was his normal jovial self. 'I'm just ringing to find out how you are. And to ask you to thank Rudi for what he's done.'

'How did you know where to find me? What do you mean? What has he done?'

'Steady on!' he laughed. 'One at a time! I knew where you were because Rudi rang me yesterday to give me your number. And he's done quite a lot. Enough to satisfy my accountant as well as bring a smile back to my bank manager's face. It's amazing what a little influence and a lot of hard cash can achieve.'

'Oh.' Arabella felt her brain rushing round in circles, but before she had time to try to sort out her thoughts his voice was continuing.

'But tell me, love, how are you feeling? Not suffering from wedding nerves, I hope.'

'Of course not.' She was determined to sound convincing. 'Not the least danger.'

'Great. Oh, and tell Rudi that I had a call from the airline to confirm our flights for next week. I'll ring Caroline later to let her know. It'll be nice to have her company on the plane. I won't tell you how early we have to leave to get there on time, but we're due in Munich at ten-thirty, and Rudi has made arrangements for us to be picked up.'

'I'm looking forward to seeing you, Dad.'

When the call had ended, Arabella replaced the receiver, stood for a few moments studying her face in the mirror above the small table. Then, uncertain what was governing her actions, she found herself taking the rose from her suit and tossing it down. Almost immediately the phone rang again, and this time her hunch that Rudi had arrived was confirmed.

Had her father's telephone call underlined the basic reason for the wedding? Something had caused her earlier excitement to evaporate, and when she went downstairs she was able to greet her fiancé with a cool little smile, to accept his kiss which might have been intended for her mouth on an averted cheek.

'You slept well?' A slanting glance when they were held up at traffic lights was tense and watchful, but at the last minute relaxed into a smile. 'You certainly look as if you did.' Admiration and a touch of something warmer flicked briefly across his face. 'I always liked you in pink.'

Inexplicably, tears stung her eyes so swiftly that she turned away from him. That was true; once he had told her that she should wear no other colour. 'Except,' he had whispered against her cheek, 'when you wear blue, or white, or lemon. In every colour you look beautiful. Not black, I think. I doubt that I would like you to wear black.' And he had shuddered dramatically as if the colour repelled him.

And yet today, wearing with dark slacks a jacket so dark as to be almost black, a black V-necked pullover and a dazzling white shirt, he looked, if not conventionally handsome, certainly positive and arresting. The kind of man most women would look at twice and would find intriguing. Arabella caught sight of his eyes in the mirror and wrenched her gaze away, reluctant to give up her slow study of the man.

'Where are you taking me?' The car had been parked and they were walking past the Kaiser Wilhelm Gedächtniskirche, she totally conscious of

his fingers, strong and possessive on her arm, eyes
averted from the spot where they had quarrelled so
bitterly that other time. The last sight she had had
of him had been there. A shudder racked her, and
his fingers tightened their grip.

'You are cold, Arabella?'

She mumbled something, shocked that he appeared to have forgotten, but at once braced herself,
determined to be thankful that at least one of them
would not be constant prey to all kinds of nostalgia.

'You were asking where we were going.' They had
passed Café Krantzler where all the *Kaffeeklatsch*
matrons in their silks and furs watched the passing
show; Rudi's pressure on her arm hurried her on
till they reached the huge plate-glass windows of
Berlin's most fashionable jeweller. Here they
paused, looking through the windows to the
incredible assortment of unusual and amusing time-
pieces. One, a study in perpetual motion, was
operated by balls rolling down ramps arranged in
all kinds of weird patterns, at last being raised by
transferred weight to begin their task again. Another
was a quaint affair of levers and ratchets which
somehow jerked the seconds away and the hands of
the clock into action. Arabella stared in fascination
until, realising Rudi was watching her absorption
with a faint smile, she transferred her attention.

'Are you going to buy a clock?' But almost as
soon as she asked the question she realised the
probable reason for their visit, and blushed.

'No.' The door was opened by a man who would
have been quite at home guarding Fort Worth. 'I'm
going to buy a ring.'

The ring they chose, after a great deal of
consideration, was a simple one; Arabella's taste
had never been for showy diamonds, but she felt
almost sentimental about the small but brilliantly
clear sapphire guarded by two diamonds, utterly
conventional, which she saw being packed into

velvet-lined boxes along with two matching wedding rings, then wrapped in the distinctive red and gold paper which was one of the hallmarks of the famous jeweller.

'I'm rather glad—' they had returned to the villa in the Grünewald for lunch and Rudi took the box from his pocket, slipping the ring on to her finger, raising her chin, staring down into her eyes and brushing his mouth against hers, 'glad you didn't take the other ring.' The salesman had been discreetly persuasive over a huge square-cut diamond. 'They suit certain kinds of film star, but not you, Arabella.' The way he spoke told her he was paying a compliment, and she made no move to withdraw when his fingers circled her neck and pulled her closer.

But that was just when Frau Fischer came to announce lunch, and the chance to exploit the tenderness of the moment was gone. But he toasted her at lunch, again in champagne, and for a time he seemed to be the amusing companion she remembered, even though he did not attempt to assume the role of lover.

The following day they were to leave for Bavaria, but Arabella, having recovered from her original pique, found there were certain things she had to buy for her wedding. Rudi had said nothing about a honeymoon, and she had no idea what kind of clothes she would require in the immediate future, so she compromised by purchasing some of everything, bowing graciously this time to Rudi's insistence that all her purchases should be charged to his accounts.

Besides, she found it rather fun to have the run of the whole of West Berlin and its wonderful collection of shops, and to know that she need not trouble to look at ticket prices. After so many years of straitened finances, when much of her considerable salary had been required to meet the expenses of the flat, it was wonderful to have this absolute binge. She even, berating herself for such stupid sentimentality, bought a new dress for the wedding—a part-worn gown was hardly suitable for any wedding, and certainly not for hers to Rudi Schlegel. It was quite plain, but the pure silk shimmered with a pearly quality which she had seldom seen, and the high neckline and cuffs were embroidered with pink seed-pearls. With it she chose a wide shady hat decorated at one side with a cluster of pink tea-roses.

'You should always wear pink.' Rudi's words kept returning to her mind, and she wondered a little tenderly if her gesture of reconciliation would be recognised. Extricating herself from the folds of the dress in the fitting-room, she paused as the meaning of the word hit her. Reconciliation. The saleswoman had withdrawn and she had the room to herself, was able to study her own reaction to the implications. The slow burn of colour in her cheeks, the sudden dryness of her mouth, the churning pitch of her stomach and . . . And, yes, the glitter of excitement in her eyes. She was going to marry Rudi. After five years apart they were going to be happy. In the end, it was bound to be so . . .

CHAPTER SEVEN

THEIR journey south, contrary to Arabella's expectation, was by car, the huge boot as well as the rear seat totally packed with the boxes of new clothes and the cases she had brought from England. First they travelled along the East German autobahn, through the various checkpoints towards Helmstedt, and then on West German soil down one of the country's main arteries.

The trip was long and tiring, and towards the end of it Arabella had to keep jerking herself awake. As if aware of her condition, Rudi pressed a button and they were enveloped by evocative soothing music, which ought to have encouraged her to drop off, but which instead thrust her back into the mood of burning resentment with which she was constantly having to struggle.

'Is Klara Steyr your favourite singer?' She didn't manage to keep the note of sarcasm from her voice. Maybe bacause she didn't try hard enough.

'One of them.' She sensed his swift sideways glance. 'You disagree with my choice?'

'No, of course not.' But before she had finished speaking Rudi had thrust out a finger towards the control and the tape changed, this time away from opera to something bland and anonymous to which she could take no exception.

'Go to sleep, Arabella.' Although he spoke reasonably, she chose to consider it an order and closed her eyes angrily. But it was impossible to maintain that position when she felt her senses begin to leave her and she went along with them, abandoning all her resentful thoughts.

When the car began to slow she awoke with a start, heard the crunch of wheels on gravel and pushed herself upright.

'We are here, Arabella.' Unexpectedly he reached out, his fingers linking with hers. 'Welcome to Schloss Möwe.' His mouth brushed on hers, seductive in the semi-darkness. A throb ran through her, but before she could respond by putting up a hand to his cheek he had moved away.

'*Schloss* . . .' Bewildered, she studied the large house with at least a dozen windows softly illuminated. 'Did you say *Schloss*?'

'I did. Not much of a castle, I'm afraid, but that's what it's always been called, since it was built away back in the eighteenth century.'

'It looks quite big enough.' By now he had come round and was helping her from the car. 'I had no idea . . .'

'I wanted to surprise you.' For just a minute he encircled her in his arms, smiling down in the way of any young man saving some special piece of news for the girl he loved. Arabella felt her heart contract, give the familiar little lurch, in the split second before he led her forward to the front door, one arm still about her waist.

Inside she was relieved to find it even less like a castle, more on the lines of a luxurious country mansion. She sensed that Rudi was watching her carefully, and made no attempt to hide her pleasure.

'But it's beautiful!' She was led from the wide hallway down a short corridor and into a room completely lined in some gold-coloured wood, several rich-looking pictures decorating the walls and glass-fronted bookshelves filled with leather-bound volumes. At each side of the door they had entered were recesses with glass shelves, each holding an attractive piece of porcelain, on one a simple bowl, while another held a china ballerina in creamy tutu, arms extended as she performed an arabesque, the whole faintly lighted from some source hidden in the ceiling.

The floor was carpeted in a soft neutral colour, and several oriental rugs were scattered about. Several chairs in various shades of green and pink, one more masculine in green leather and brass studded, together with occasional tables dotted around, completed the furnishings. Arabella moved towards a wide window embrasure and looked out on to a shadowy garden before turning again to Rudi, arms raised for a moment before she allowed them to drop helplessly to her sides.

'I . . . I had no idea you would live in a place like this. The Grünewald house is grand enough, but this . . .'

Without replying he walked forward and opened a door on the far wall, and then with a murmured excuse he left for a few moments.

'*Mutti.*' Almost at once he returned with an elderly woman, nearly as tall as Arabella, and the resemblance between mother and son was quite striking, in spite of her abundant and elegantly coiffed white hair. 'This is Arabella. *Liebchen*, I want you to meet my mother.'

'Arabella.' The warmth in the woman's voice made the girl weak and trembly, as if unexpectedly a lifetime's longing for a mother might be fulfilled, and she found that her offered hand was used to pull her into a warm embrace. '*So* much about you have I heard.' She spoke English fairly well but with a strong accent. 'And so delighted am I to welcome you to our home.' She kissed the girl on both cheeks before looking at her son, saying something in German which Arabella didn't catch but which brought a smile to her son's lips, even a softening in his glance as he nodded agreement.

'Mother is saying,' his attitude towards his fiancée

was warmer than it had yet been, 'that I did not exaggerate one bit when I . . . told her of you.'

'Not one bit,' the old lady concurred heartily. 'Now we shall go into the other room and ring for some tea. I know that is what you will want after your journey. Lise has all afternoon been waiting your arrival; I cannot think how she missed you. But,' she pressed a concealed button to summon the maid, waved the newcomer to a seat and took one herself, 'when you have had tea you must rest until dinner, when I shall tell you all the arrangements we have made for the wedding. Such a rush!' She looked reprovingly at her son who lounged over the back of Arabella's chair, tut-tutted, then smiled. 'But now that I have seen her I understand completely your impatience. Now,' there was a rattle of crockery, the bump of a tea trolley from the direction of the corridor, 'you will meet our Lise—more a friend than a servant. The best creature who ever lived.'

Lise, a lined but strong-faced woman in her mid-fifties, remained with them in the room, joining them for tea and subjecting Arabella to a very critical examination and several searching questions while plying her with a substantial assortment of sandwiches and cakes, most of which she felt obliged to try.

'That was delicious.' At last she put down her plate with a firm little gesture which dissuaded further efforts at persuasion. 'I must have put on *pounds* of weight with all those cream cakes; they're all so tempting.'

'I'm sure you need not worry, my dear.' Frau von Schlegel, who seemed herself not to have a spare ounce of flesh, cast a critical eye over her. 'Besides . . .' Whatever she was about to say was arrested as she caught her son's eye, and she immediately busied herself with plates and cups.

But Arabella, with an immediate understanding

of what Rudi's mother had been about to say, felt a
wave of colour hit her cheeks. It was so easy to
read the older woman's mind. Besides, she must
have been about to say, you'll be having a baby
soon and your figure won't matter.

The idea that everyone knew his reasons for
marrying made her blaze with angry humiliation,
and the glance she directed at her fiancé was
designed to inform him of her feelings. Apart from
a slight narrowing of his eyes, she could not be
entirely certain he had got the message, and that
was doubly irritating.

When she reached the bedroom Arabella found
her case and bags already there, piled on the rack
at the foot of the bed, apparently delivered by the
unobtrusive staff who ran the house with such
impeccable efficiency. Doubtless they worked under
Lise's direction, her role of housekeeper overlapping
that of family friend and companion to Rudi's
mother, but whatever the position, it seemed to
Arabella that after marriage her domestic duties
would not impose too much of a burden.

She was just reaching into her bag for her keys
when a tap at the door signalled the arrival of a
young woman, smiling and friendly, but who
demonstrated dismay, when she saw the guest begin
to unpack, insisting that was her job. As she went
about her work she chatted, admiring all the clothes
which she shook out and hung in the fitted wardrobe
which covered one entire wall of the bedroom,
looking pleased when Arabella, using the same mix
of German and English, praised the *Schloss*
generously.

Who could do otherwise, thought Arabella when
at last she was left alone in the room and felt free
to kick off her shoes and lie down on the bed, when
it was just about the most luxurious house she had
ever seen? This bedroom, for example: three floor-
length windows looked out over the grounds, filmy

white curtains stirred in the faint breeze, and later on the heavy silk drapes, pink like the bedhead and banded with gold, would be pulled to exclude the world.

Dissatisfied with herself, disturbed by the direction of her thoughts, Arabella rose in one smooth movement and went to the bathroom where she watched water foam into the large tub. Extravagantly she tossed in several capfuls of scented oil and then, with a sigh of relief, climbed in for a leisurely soak. But she found that the warmth of the water, the scents which rose disturbingly in her nostrils, forced her mind back along the lines which she wished she could avoid . . .

How would she cope when she and Rudi were alone in the house together? During her conversation with his mother, it had been made clear that the older woman and Lise would be moving shortly to a house nearby, a plan which had been in preparation even before news of the sudden wedding had broken.

'Most young men don't want two old women watching every move, checking on his friends, so we have been meaning to move, and last year we found the perfect little house for us. Your coming, my dear, means we can leave with an easy mind'— here Frau von Schlegel leaned forward and touched the girl's knee—'knowing how happy he will be.'

But that, thought Arabella as she lay in the warm water, eyes closed, was something that would not follow automatically. Feeling as she did, knowing what she did, tormented by the sight of him, longing for him to act with the old impetuosity, she doubted whether it was within her power to bring him any happiness or peace. Not when she was longing for him to behave as if he were in love with her even if . . . even if she were merely substituting for Klara.

Yes, that was the rub. Opening her eyes, she

gazed mournfully up at the array of expensive
creams and powders on the shelf at the end of the
bath. How should she conceal her own feelings,
when all the time she felt he would have preferred
to be making love to someone else? To Klara Steyr.

The pain caused by such contemplations was so
great that she pulled on the lever and let all the
deliciously scented water flow away. But at least it
helped concentrate her mind in one direction, made
her determine that she would not accept the fact of
her husband's mistress without putting up a fight.
She could not sing as entrancingly as Klara, that
was one field where she could not compete, but in
other ways she could give her a run for her money.

And the sight of so many pretty dresses when she
threw open the door of the wardrobe made her
realise that the battle had not yet started. A tiny
giggle, nervous but excited, extended the smile as
she wondered just what would be her first shot. If
fine feathers and artifice could do anything to help
then no one was more expert in their use than
Arabella Smythe.

By the time she had descended the staircase, all
her self-confidence had returned, helped in no small
measure by the dress bought in one of Berlin's most
exclusive shops, horrendously expensive but worth
every Mark she, or rather Rudi, had paid for it.
The soft reseda-green was perfect with her colouring,
and the plain lines of the dress, piped round the
dropped shoulders and on the bracelet cuffs in
cinnamon satin, showed her long figure to perfection.
Cut on the bias, it clung softly above the waist,
while the fluid material belled about her legs as she
walked.

Expertly she had chosen the right make-up to
complement the colours, soft beigey-pink eye
shadow with pearly bronze lipstick, her long lashes
just emphasised with a flick of gilt mascara. High-
heeled sandals in gold snakeskin took her just an

inch higher than usual, so when Rudi walked to the foot of the stairs to greet her, she had to raise her eyes only a little to meet his gaze.

And the expression she met brought her heart to a rapid tattoo beneath her ribs, so reminiscent was it of the way he had once admired her without words. And the tender way he took her fingers to his lips while looking at her face was far from calming. Was it simply that she was so unused to it? she wondered in panic. Or was it because this was Rudi Schlegel, this was Arabella Smythe?

'*Du bist . . . wunderschön.*' A second after he spoke he smiled ruefully, shrugged his shoulders lightly. 'A writer ought to be able to do so much better!'

During dinner, served by the apparently indispensable Lise, although this seemed to be one meal she took apart from the family, much of the conversation centred on plans for the wedding, now only two days away. Although Rudi's mother deferred a great deal, asking her opinion and advice on all kinds of minor details, it was obvious to Arabella that things had already been arranged with considerable efficiency, that there was little she could suggest which had not already been dealt with.

They had reached the dessert when Lise murmured something to Frau von Schlegel. Arabella caught the '*Blumen*', but she was finding that her ear for German had gone, and both woman spoke with accents more than a little strange.

'*Ach, ja.*' The older woman nodded. '*Danke,* Lise.' Her smile encompassed the other two. 'She has just reminded me . . . What of the flowers for the reception, Arabella? Already Rudi has spoken to me about them, but . . .' her glance at her son was tender, not quite adoring, '. . . men do not always understand these things. As I said'—for some reason Arabella felt an increasing warmth in her cheeks, and looked down at her plate as if the

slicing of a peach required mathematical precision—
'we shall receive the guests in the salon and the
wedding lunch will be laid out in the dining-room,
with tables in the garden so our guests can sit out if
the weather is fine. But it would be pleasant if we
could match the flowers in the house with your
dress, and flowers you might be carrying.'

'I . . .' It was ridiculous to be staring at her plate,
like some gauche kind of girl instead of a woman in
her twenties, so Arabella made the effort and raised
her head, pointedly ignoring her fiancé but finding
an attractive smile for Frau von Schlegel. 'I hadn't
thought of carrying flowers, I imagined we would
have a very quiet wedding. Just the civil ceremony,
then lunch for a few friends.'

'*Natürlich*, a small wedding. That does not mean
we should not make things as charming as possible.
Besides,' her tone was mildly teasing, 'I have just
one son, no daughter, and shall not have another
opportunity to plan a wedding, so you must allow
me some indulgence.'

'Of course.' Inadvertently Arabella had allowed
herself to look towards Rudi and sensed a very
powerful warning in his eyes, a look that made her
feel resentment but one which she could not possibly
ignore. She flicked her eyes back to his mother.
'Well, there are some pink roses on my hat.'

'There!' Frau von Schlegel smiled in triumph.
'Exactly what Rudi said. He promised me you
would wear pink flowers, and . . .'

'Really?' Her cold eyes invited him to explain
just why he should imagine he had the entrée into
her thoughts.

'Yes.' Frau von Schlegel's attention was taken up
by the removal of things from the table; she pushed
back her chair with a sigh, extending her arm
towards Arabella to indicate that she too should
rise. 'We shall take the *Kaffee* in the other room.
He assured me,' as she slipped her hand into

Arabella's arm she cast a teasing glance at her son who followed them, 'that you would choose pink, and that is exactly what we have ordered. They could easily be changed, of course, but it would have caused a little trouble, and I . . .'

'There was no chance of that, *Mutti*.' They had reached the small sitting-room which was used most of the time. Arabella, at one end of a sofa trying to be unaware of Rudi at the far end, watched coffee being poured. He reached for a cup, offering it to his fiancée, his fingers holding on to the saucer till she was forced to look up with an angry, questioning expression. 'As I told you, Arabella always looks her best in pink.'

'In that case,' she spoke in a low voice which she hoped would not carry clearly to the woman opposite, 'my wedding dress is going to be a great disappointment to you.' Her tone was intended to convey that much more than the mere dress was going to give him cause for complaint, then she leaned forward to discuss some further details of the arrangments for the reception.

However, as soon as she could, Arabella made the excuse of fatigue and, scarcely waiting for a reaction from either of them, left the room, running swiftly up the wide staircase, feeling vulnerable until she had reached her bedroom and had closed the door firmly behind her. Her eyes moved round the room as if she were in some kind of luxurious trap, then a cynical smile twisted her lips.

If it were a trap, then surely it was one which many women would be only too happy to occupy. In fact—levering herself away from the door, she gave a shuddering sigh—she was about to embark on the most advantageous marriage she could have dreamed of, besides it being the only man whom she had ever dreamed of. If only, if *only* this persisent image of Klara would go away . . . Even this evening, when she had run downstairs determined to make him forget Klara, she had discovered that was something *she* was finding impossible to wipe from her mind. And when memories of the great diva flooded in then she heard herself becoming offhand and shrewish, the reverse of what she intended. Oh . . . She would just have to try harder, that was all. Impatiently she reached for the long zip at her back, pulled it down so she could step out of her dress and . . .

A swift rap at the door interrupted her semi-coherent thoughts and she whirled round as the door opened and Rudi stepped inside, closing it as she had done a moment earlier by leaning against it. But he was far from being the man she had left downstairs, further still from the fanciful image she had just been remembering. Fury blazed in the dark eyes, and there was menace in the sudden step he took towards her.

One of her hands moved in an involuntary fashion towards her throat, till she remembered and pretended to play with the thin gold chain about her neck. 'You wanted something?' Lacking the courage to continue the faintly baiting mood she had shown downstairs, still she was not prepared to soften completely. Not unless . . .

'You could say that.' His glance dismissed any idea he might just have wanted her. 'I wanted to tell you that I would not tolerate such childish behaviour as you showed downstairs, and to warn you against any repetition.' He saw her lips tighten, flicked a contemptuous look over her face. 'And don't trouble to deny your behaviour, for we both know what you were doing.'

'And why?' With an effort she turned, walked with unhurried steps which she prayed would hide her agitation; it was an effort to stop herself reaching out for the dressing-gown which lay the foot of her bed. 'We both know why!' Reaching the dressing-table, she paused, extending her fingers to look at them, and began to pull the ring from her hand.

'Why doesn't come into it.' Instantly he come up behind her, his sudden appearance in the mirror making her lashes flick open to reveal her dismay. His fingers took her by the shoulders, swung her round so she could be in no doubt of his reactions to her attitude. 'We had an agreement, a contract. I expect you keep your side, the spirit as well as the letter.'

'Oh, I'll keep my part.' Arabella choked back a sob. 'Don't worry about that.'

'Then you'll have to do a great deal better than you did tonight. I have no intention of allowing my mother to be upset by your stupid behaviour. She imagines we are marrying for the usual reasons, and I'm determined she at least will not be disillusioned. Just as I shall do my best to see that your father does not get the idea that you are marrying me simply to get him out of his financial difficulties. I expect you to play your part.'

'Maybe,' she was stung to reply, 'I'm not such a good actor as you are.'

'Then,' his voice was hard and hateful and as he spoke he pulled her a little closer to him, 'you'll just have to practise, won't you.'

And before she could even think what he was meaning, his mouth had closed on hers. Shock and outrage were her only excuses for what happened then. For instead of hardening against him, her lips softened, parted expectantly, so even the savagery of his onslaught became an insidious delight, a joy which burned through her body, obliterating the bitterness of the years. And without thinking she responded, standing on tiptoe so their bodies could blend more intimately, reaching with her hands for the nape of his neck, excited by the soft tangle of hair against her fingers.

Then, as if he too were beguiled by an unexpected

response, the fierceness left him, his mouth became
as warm and gentle as she ever remembered and,
feeling the press of the bed against the back of her
legs, she allowed herself to subside, pulling him
down with her. A soft moan reached her ears—his,
her own—it was impossible to say—but as if he
were encouraged his kiss deepened. Arabella felt
the world and all its problems begin to spin away
from her as her body became absorbed in a whirling
spiral of pleasure.

Rudi's fingers had slipped the slender straps from
her shoulders, his mouth left hers to search for the
throbbing pulse at her throat, to seek the deep cleft
of her breasts. Then both her hands were captured
in one of his, held above her on the pillows while
he gazed down for a moment, totally absorbing the
tumbled hair, eyes half closed, lips parted, the
heaving bosom barely constrained by the wisps of
fragile silk and lace.

Shuddering, she arched against him, and in willing
complicity his free hand slipped beneath her thighs
and she was held in pulsing intimate contact while
his mouth resumed its slow potent plunder of hers.
Again that moan, plaintive, yielding, reached her
ears, and at the same time she heard his voice
repeating her name as if it were a litany.

How long it continued she had no idea; time
ceased to hold any meaning for her, but she knew
that the sounds of pleasure were coming from her
own lips. Then, feeling him roll away from her, she
opened her eyes and discovered him looking down
at her with a strange yet familiar expression on his
face. His hair was dishevelled, his breathing agitated,
but there was a slight curve to his mouth that
signalled amusement.

He rose, offering her a hand which pulled her to
her feet and into his embrace again. 'You see, *mein
Schätzchen*,' the very word wiped out the years of
estrangement and indifference, 'it is as I thought.'

The hint of humour persisted in the gleaming eyes. 'A little practice will make a world of difference. And only the fact that our wedding is so near prevents me continuing the lessons now.'

He raked back the hair from his forehead, then, raising her fingers to his lips, kissed then lightly. A moment later Arabella was alone in the bedroom.

CHAPTER EIGHT

'Hi, Bella.' Caroline erupted into the bedroom with all the finesse of a tornado, making Arabella turn round with that wild tattoo of her pulses which was becoming all too familiar, subsiding quickly when she realised it was only her best friend. 'Here I am, at the last minute as usual.' She wrapped her arms about the girl by the window. 'I was terrified I was going to miss your wedding.'

'That would have been ghastly!' Arabella's words were slightly more heartfelt than she realised. 'It would have been awful to be married with none of my friends here. Did . . .' She bit fiercely at her lower lip, turning to hide her expression, unaware that the tremble in her voice was as much a give-away as any look would have been. 'Did Dad come with you?'

'Of *course*.' Caroline threw herself on to the bed, looking round approvingly. 'I'm impressed, love.' One hand smoothed the quilted silk cover. 'You're doing very well for yourself.'

'Oh, that's not why . . .' The half-lie was automatic.

'Of course not, you idiot,' Caroline laughed, and got up. 'Didn't we always promise each other that we'd marry only for love? But we did always keep our fingers crossed that there would be some money too. Lucky you.'

'But . . .'

'I *know*. I *know* you're crazy about Rudi. And so would I be if he had looked in my direction. If only,' she sighed dramatically, laying a hand on her heart, 'if only Kulu had taken me to that reception instead of you.'

'But,' now that she had recovered her poise, Arabella was able to adopt the same teasing note, 'I was going to say when you interrupted, don't forget I knew Rudi years and years ago and . . .'

'Yes, I know,' Caroline affected cynicism, 'when you were both young. But anyway, I must go. I just dashed up to ask if it was all right for your father to come up now. I understand you're confined to your room till it's time to leave for the registrar or whatever they call themselves here. Papa wants to know if you're decent.' She cast a quick professional eye over her friend's mimosa silk housecoat. 'I'll tell him yes. Then if you want me to come up and help you dress . . .'

Arabella giggled. 'I can never understand this assumption that a woman suddenly becomes so helpless on her wedding day that she's unable to dress herself. I've been managing to do just that for all of my life, and . . .'

'You're supposed to be too nervy to fasten up your buttons and things.' Caroline got to her feet, walked to the dressing-table and picked up a pot of face cream. 'Do you think this stuff does any good? Oh, never mind . . . I'd better go. Shall I come up later or not?'

'Of course I want you to come up. But do forgive me if I don't allow you to dress me.' By then they were both giggling, but when she was alone Arabella had to fight the sting of tears at the back of her eyes. Her wedding day. It was the first time she had admitted to herself that it had actually arrived. In spite of all the fuss about her staying in her room in case the bridegroom should catch just a glimpse of his bride, the glimpse which would spell inevitable disaster for the marriage, in spite of the smiles and cosseting she had endured from Frau von Schlegel and Lise, only with Caroline's arrival came the total realisation that there was no escape. In less than two hours' time she was going to marry Rudi.

There was a firm knock on the door and her father's head appeared round the door.

'Daddy!' She flew to him, and the instant his arms closed round her there was no longer a need to suppress the tears that cascaded down her cheeks.

By the time she had dressed she was perfectly in control of her emotions. The long talk with her father, during which he had demanded and received assurances that her rushed marriage had nothing to do with his shaky commercial affairs, had done much to strengthen her resolve, to convince her that she wasn't about to make the greatest mistake of her life. In spite of her father's bad judgment when it came to choosing his own friends and business associates, it was important to her that he should approve her choice, and that he did heartily within seconds of arriving.

Tears threatened again when, just before leaving his daughter to complete her preparations, he took hold of her arms, staring down, blue eyes filled with all the affection he had always given. 'And don't think, darling, that it's just because Rudi's helped me out of a mess that I have such a high opinion of him. For he's exactly the kind of man I would have chosen for you—not that,' a sudden smile lightened a fraught moment, 'girls these days even think of letting their fathers have a say in the matter.' He gave her a tiny shake. 'But anyone can see he's crazy about you.'

'Really?' Her only hope of retaining some self-control was to enter into the spirit of the conversation. 'Now, how can you tell such a thing when you haven't even seen us together?'

'No, but I have seen his expression when he mentions your name. Besides, how could any man help being madly in love with you? The only thing that surprises me is that you haven't been whirled off to the altar long before this. But now that I've met Rudi, I'm beginning to understand even that. And now,' he bent to kiss her cheek, 'I'm going to call Caroline for you. She insists that she won't put on her dress until she's made sure you're all right. You know, I think she has designs on the best man. There was a distinct gleam in her eye when they were introduced. I wonder if I ought to go down and warn him.'

'Don't *dare!*' Arabella was laughing as she turned away and her lips were still curving upwards when Caroline arrived to check on the bride.

'Oh, Bella!' When she had completed the few necessary adjustments, Caroline sat back on her heels on the carpet looking up at her friend with a rapt, dreamy expression quite at variance with the blasé image she normally tried to promote. 'You look absolutely heavenly. I swear, when Kulu sees the photographs he'll be green that he didn't design your dress.'

'There was no time for that, but I'm glad you like it.' In spite of her offhand reaction, Arabella could not resist sidelong glances in the long mirror which stood in one corner of the room, glances which were a total confirmation of Caroline's opinion. It did look gorgeous, the fluid lines and the luxurious softness of the silk combining to make the most of a near-perfect figure, sleeves tight from wrist to elbow then with an Edwardian fullness. And her change of hairstyle, loosely bundled on top of her head, suited the hat which dipped low over her forehead in a provocative way, not totally in keeping with the aspect of bridal innocence she ought to have been trying to project, but adding a hint of mischief to the occasion. In fact, excitement kept rising up inside her, smudgy dark eyes blazed back at her and then, remembering she was not alone, a

flick of long lashes concealed her expression and
she paid attention to something Caroline was saying.

'I must dash. I've only to slip on my dress and fix
my hair and face properly. Wasn't it lucky I bought
that peach dress and you remembered how perfectly
it would tone with yours? I . . .'

'Yes, hurry, Caroline. You know your room,
across the landing and down the corridor; Lise
showed me yesterday.'

'I'm just sorry I have to rush back tonight. Only I
have this session tomorrow afternoon. Anyway,'
reaching the door, she turned for a final word,
'your dad is anxious to get back too, so it's just as
well . . . See you in about ten minutes . . .'

The door closed as Arabella turned away from
the mirror towards the window. In Caroline's
language ten minutes could hardly be less than
twenty, so it was as well they had lots of time in
hand. Down below, a whole army of helpers were
setting out small tables on the lawns, but she was
too absorbed by her own emotional state to pay
them much attention.

And then she had a sudden panic, remembering
that she had forgotten to borrow something from
Caroline, and it was a tradition she dare not ignore.
It might be just the talisman which would save both
of them from a life of married unhappiness. Without
thinking any further, she found herself running
soundlessly across the landing, turning into the
short corridor leading to the bedrooms in the west
wing.

But not until she reached the partially opened
door of his room did she remember that that was
where Rudi's bedroom was situated, that in this
stupid, superstitious search for good luck she was in
great danger of encountering the bridegroom, which
everyone agreed was horrendously *un*lucky. So
unlucky that no number of borrowed handkerchiefs
would be likely to deflect it. In half-amused

excitement, exaggerating the danger in her own mind, she held her breath, suddenly flattening herself against the wall as his voice, speaking rapidly in his own language, came towards her. It was easy to imagine him striding about the room, exchanging last-minute jokes with his best man—presumably bridegrooms as well as brides had to be supervised—she could *see* him reaching for his jacket, shrugging the powerful shoulders into the dark cloth, turning to adjust his tie. Her heart gave a crazy little leap and . . .

. . . And then she was recognising something special in his tone and manner, something which indicated that whoever he was addressing, it was not one of his own sex. Now the beating of her heart was sheer agitation, and inadvertently her fingers went up to suppress the cry that burst from her lips, oblivious to pain as the stones from her ring cut into her soft cheek, listening to the beguiling, persuasive voice of his companion.

Klara Steyr's voice could not be mistaken. It had a rich, throbbing quality which distinguished it from any other and now, charged as it was with some deeply held emotion, it forced Arabella to strain so she could discern the words.

'Rudi,' there was a strong hint of tears, of pleading, 'you cannot mean it, that after your marriage . . .'

'*Natürlich, mein Schätzchen* . . .' That endearment which she had thought was hers alone . . . The flow of conversation faded as Arabella tried to control her own despair; voices became lower, she moved forward a little, despising herself even as she did so, not now trying to subdue her bitterness as her worst suspicions were confirmed.

It was merely a corner of mirror, visible from the doorway, that relayed the whole story. Rudi had his arms about the woman, his head was bending low towards her upturned lips. As she whirled silently away, a gurgling, satisfied laugh followed her, telling her that Klara was content with what she had achieved.

Alone in her bedroom, Arabella allowed all rational behaviour to flood away from her, caring nothing of the consequences of what she was about to do. In fact, sunk in agonising despair as she was, she only half realised what was happening; fingers tearing at buttons and fastenings were following no coherent plan, were merely the reaction to over-taut emotions suddenly snapping.

It wasn't sufficient to discard the dress, she had to throw it from her in disgust, the matching petticoat joining it in a pile in the corner of the room. For a second she stood shivering, arms wrapped about herself, oblivious now of any reflection and the stricken beauty she portrayed.

Then, still with the same feverish haste, she wrenched at the door of her wardrobe, blank eyes searching for . . . for what? She couldn't think. Yet there was a throb of triumph as her hand reached out, slid from a hanger one particular dress. It would be ideal for the occasion, perfect for her views of marriage in general, her own in particular.

A moment later she had pulled the skimpy thing over her head, shaking fingers were reaching for the long back-zip, she drew a shuddering sigh as she turned to face the result. Black cotton knit, cut straight across at the neck, clinging to the figure until it ended six inches above the knee. It looked quite dreadful, and she couldn't remember why she had taken it to Berlin, apart from some forewarned inspiration. Maybe she had thought she might go swimming in the Wannsee and it was comfortable to slip on over a bikini. Its soft touch on the skin was its only virtue.

But still . . . Momentarily her heart failed as she imagined the result of what she was planning. Not only Rudi, she positively wanted to hurt him, but . . . his mother? Her father? Caroline? Lise and all the family friends? Oh no, she couldn't. *Couldn't*!

A sudden rap at the door took her whirling round to face it. A hand went protectively to the curve of her breast as she braced herself to meet Caroline's dismay. And when the door opened a mist came down over her eyes, cleared as Rudi materialised in front of her.

His gentleness of expression lasted less than a second before it was swept away in a look of quite lacerating shock and coldness, the dark eyes flicking over, taking in every detail of the ghastly dress before coming to rest with quite frightening intensity on her face. Then he took a step towards her, paused, eyebrows pulled together in demonic arches, his mouth a thin ugly line.

Briefly he turned away, Arabella saw one hand reach out to the key and they were locked in the room. As he turned back she saw what had apparently brought him to her room; a posy of creamy pink rosebuds, fringed with maidenhair fern and curls of narrow ribbon in amber satin, arched away from him, leaving his fingers free to take her shoulders and shake her furiously. 'What in God's name do you think you're doing?'

'Wh–what do you mean?' It was useless to pretend she wasn't frightened. She was. And with reason. Behind the coldness of his eyes was terrible anger that hovered on the verge of violence. And here was she, locked in the bedroom with him. She watched him glance quickly about, saw his eyes alight on the tumbled wedding clothes before returning to contemplate her again.

'Take off that dress at once!'

'Don't talk to me like that, or . . .'

At the same time he bared his teeth at her, savage fingers were ripping at the zipper and he was pulling the garment from her shoulders. Arabella gave a tiny whimper, crossed her arms protectively in an attempt to conceal her barely clad figure, and felt a sting of humiliation when he laughed grimly.

'You need not worry, *mein Schätzchen.*' Had she ever thought the endearment tender, irresistible? His hands were raising the creamy dress and underskirt, holding them out to her. 'You have never been safer than you are now at this minute.' Another humourless smile. 'At least your virtue is totally safe.' His tone suggested her life might not be. 'Now,' he rasped, 'get into that dress.'

'I . . . I . . .'

'Don't argue!' As he spoke he began to pull the underskirt over her head, and almost instinctively she raised her arms to thrust them into the armholes. 'I don't mind,' with total disregard for her skin he pulled roughly at the zipper, 'what you do to me. You can humiliate me as much as you like, but I'm not prepared to let you ruin my mother's peace of mind. She's had little enough in the last years, and no spoiled little brat is going to rob her of this day.' Now they had reached the dress, and his hands were so strong and forceful that she feared for the delicate material. 'After this . . . farce is over we'll have all the time in the world to tear each other to shreds, but today . . . you'll act as you've never done before. Have you got that?' To emphasise his question he spun her round, took her by the shoulders and gave her another shake, unmoved by the tears which welled up in her eyes.

'And,' with an effort she stifled both tears and the sobs which kept rising in her throat, 'and if I don't?'

'If you don't,' he bent close so the astringent scent of his aftershave rose in her nostrils, 'then your father will be ruined just as easily as that.' The snap of his fingers was accompanied by an unpleasant smile. 'It's still not too late.'

He didn't trouble to turn as the door behind him rattled and they heard Caroline's voice calling.

'Tell her,' he spoke softly, 'that you are just coming.'

Hypnotised by his expression, Arabella heard her voice doing as he told her. There was the faintest quiver as she spoke, and she turned blindly from him, putting on her hat without even glancing at the mirror.

'Right?' His voice had softened not a jot as he reached behind him for the key. Then, as he swung open the door, he laughed at Caroline's scandalised expression as if he were genuinely amused, and cleverly feigned a little contrition.

'I'm so sorry, Caroline. I just couldn't resist seeing her. And bringing her these, of course.' He held out the simple bouquet. 'With my love.' Of course Arabella was aware of the hollow mockery of his last words, but even she was shocked by the cruelty that made him lean forward and kiss her. With lips hard and cold as ice.

It was a perfectly lovely wedding. All the guests agreed, and Arabella, seeing the joy and happiness shown by her father and . . . her mother-in-law, threw herself with hectic intensity into the role that had been forced upon her. Afterwards . . . well, her mind could not cope with that just yet. Later, later when they were alone in the great house—it had been decided that the honeymoon would be postponed for a few days, and with that in mind Frau Schlegel and Lise were to depart with the other guests, leaving the newlyweds to the unobtrusive care of servants who came in daily from the village—later she would have to try to think what to do. The thought brought a shiver of apprehension.

'You are cold, my dear child.' Frau von Schlegel put out a hand and clasped hers. 'And how pale you seem! Pale but beautiful,' she added, as if her words might have given offence. 'Now . . . where is your husband?' In mock disapproval she looked round for her son. 'Leaving you so soon!'

And where would he be but with Klara Steyr, thought Arabella balefully as she saw him turn in response to his mother's call. It hardly mattered that several other people were with him; his expression was all that could be expected from a man on his wedding day, only the cold glitter as he looked directly at her telling that he had noted her reaction and that she should be careful.

So the hand round her waist pulling her close was doubly offensive, only she dared not resist, and looked up into his face, smiling in a way that deceived everyone but him.

'Rudi, Arabella is cold; she has been shivering. Why don't you'—the moment Arabella had been dreading, which he as well as she had been avoiding, was being forced upon them—'dance with your bride? It is'—for just a second the old voice quavered—'what we have all been waiting for.'

And as if at a prearranged signal the quartet which had been playing unobtrusively at the far end of the room launched into a tune, familiar enough, achingly so, but which Arabella could not have named to save her life.

Not that she particularly wanted to. All she must try for was to get through this one day and see all their guests leave. What would happen after that, she neither knew nor cared, and in the meantime it was enough to cope with this one dance, for everyone had formed a circle, smiling and waiting for them to start.

Rudi. He had never looked more handsome, and no one seeing them could possibly guess what lay behind that tenderly smiling mouth. One of his hands clasped her about the waist, the other took hers, and she was pulled close against him.

'Wh . . .' Her breast was heaving from suppressed

emotion, her brain ceased to function. 'Wh–what is it? This dance, I mean.'

'It's a waltz, *mein Schätzchen*.' White teeth gleamed as if he were amused. 'Just follow me. Quarter turns until we are both giddy with happiness.' And the entrancing melody grew louder, washing over her until she was no longer aware of what she was doing. At first slowly, then with rapidly increasing tempo, he whirled her round the floor.

Yes, everyone agreed it was a most elegant affair, the singing by the famous soprano of some of the most beautiful love songs in the language adding a fairytale note which was most appropriate at this particular marriage, adding that little bit of distinction so often lacking. No one but the bride appeared to be aware of a note of stridency in the gorgeous voice, and she naturally said nothing.

It was well into the evening when the last of the guests were ready to leave the Schloss, and Arabella had to keep tight hold of herself, struggling against the temptation to throw herself into her father's arms and beg him to take her back to London when he left with Caroline. Instead, she allowed herself to be kissed, even tried to harden herself against the suspicious brightness of his eyes as he turned and walked to the door.

'Thank you for asking me, Bella.' Caroline kissed her briefly then, turning to Rudi, she threw her arms round his neck. 'And thank you, Rudi, for this most beautiful present.' She slid back the wide sleeve of her jacket to display the platinum bracelet on her slender wrist. 'It's quite the most gorgeous piece of jewellery I've ever had, and I'll treasure it always.'

Rudi seemed amused, responded to her kiss with more warmth than his wife thought necessary. 'I believe Gunther is taking you to the airport and that you have told Heinrich he won't be required.'

'Yes.' Caroline grinned impishly. 'Gunther takes his duties as best man seriously, and says there's no need to take your chauffeur out of his way. Besides, the airport's on his way home, he said.'

'Only,' teased Rudi, 'if he goes via Switzerland.'

'Well,' Caroline shrugged, 'perhaps he really wanted to take Bella's father to the airport.'

'Very likely.'

'Oh, I must rush. They're waiting. Goodbye, darling.' Unexpectedly Caroline's eyes filled with tears. 'Bless you both, and I hope you'll always be as happy as you are today. Oh, and *do* ask me over for a weekend some time. I think I might even start learning German!' And with a final wave she disappeared inside the car which was already revving up.

Frau von Schlegel was the last to leave, and again Arabella had the absurd longing to hang on to her mother-in-law, to contradict all the plans that had been made, to beg her not to leave her alone with the man she had just married. But of course she merely allowed herself to be kissed, her smile trying to quench all the guilt she was experiencing as she decided that the old lady's pleasure in the marriage would be shattered soon enough.

'Thank you for having the waltz, Arabella. It was played at my own wedding all those years ago.' Tears glinted in the eyes so strikingly like her son's. 'Strauss's *Gold and Silver Waltz*. I shall always remember that you played it for me. You looked so perfect together. *Ach . . .*' She grew impatient with herself. 'Tears on such a day! It is because I am so happy; always, you see, have I wanted a daughter. You and I will be great friends, I know. But now,' swiftly she kissed them both, 'Lise is waiting, and you are anxious to be alone. Goodbye, my dears, Oh, and don't worry if I should stay an extra month in Baden-Baden; I'm sure it will be extremely beneficial to my arthritis. Besides, I should prefer the builders to have finished with my *Häuschen* before Lise and I move in.'

'Goodbye, *Mutti*.' Rudi was as ever tender and considerate towards his mother. In fact, seeing the way he put his arm about her, Arabella was seized by a feeling which in any other circumstances she might have construed as jealousy. But that was too ridiculous. This pain in her chest was anger, humiliation, maybe even a tincture of fear—but jealousy? How could you feel jealous of a man whom you despised so utterly.

Nevertheless, when she had stood with him in the doorway, watching the lights of the large car sweep down the drive and out through the gates, disappearing behind the hedge of aspens which ensured the house its privacy, Arabella could not ignore the tension mounting to an almost physical presence between them. And the heavy door swung to with a clang that was additionally ominous, and she was just a step ahead of Rudi as they crossed the hall.

'I think,' she paused with one foot on the first step, hand apparently resting on the banister but in fact clutching desperately, 'I'll go up and change.'

'*Ja*.' As he spoke he reached out to a small silver box on a side table, took out a cigarette and put it to his lips. Above the small flame from the lighter his eyes were impassive but watchful, so intense it was impossible to wrench her own away. 'I think you should do that, my beautiful bride.' She hardly realised what he was doing till she felt her hand brushed by his lips, she drew a painful breath. And then . . . noticed one of the servants pass almost soundlessly from one side of the hall to the other, knew from his expression of cynical amusement that the little scene had been enacted for her benefit.

Abruptly she snatched her hand away, disregarding the fact that he made no attempt to hold it, but his expression had changed. 'Don't be too long; dinner will be served in the small room to the left of the salon.'

'I . . .' Fiercely she bit her lip. 'I don't want any dinner. I'm not hungry.'

'Nonsense.' The steely look belied the slow tenderness in his voice. 'You ate hardly any lunch. All that wonderful food and you simply pushed it round your plate.'

'I wasn't hungry then; I'm not hungry now. And I'm tired, so I hope you will excuse me.' She turned to go, but before she could do more than raise herself on to the first step he had caught again at her hand.

'Of course I shall not excuse you. The servants have gone to a great deal of trouble to cook a special meal for us. For myself, I could well do without your company this evening, but they would undoubtedly be disappointed. So I must ask you to exert yourself. For their sake, you understand. Not for mine.'

As he spoke he released her, but Arabella found herself unable to move from the spot. And in the meantime he took the opportunity to look her over, from top to toe, a slow, deliberate assessment which doubtless was meant to remind her just how much he had paid for her, that he intended to get some return for his investment. A slow burn started in the pit of her stomach, quickly inflaming her whole body.

With immense effort she subdued her instinct to raise her hand and bring it down on his face. But she had no intention of descending to the gutter, so instead she raised her chin in a gesture of defiance. 'Very well.' And slowly but firmly she began to climb the stairs, forcing her legs to obey the messages from her brain, and each inch of the way she was conscious of his eyes boring into her, just as she had been that very first night at Frau Steffan's. Only this time she refused him the satisfaction that her turning round would doubtless have afforded.

When she reached her room her condition was very close to total collapse. She sank on to the stool in front of the dressing-table, wryly astonished to see that she looked . . . well, normal, if you could ignore the trappings of her recent wedding. Deathly pale, of course, but surprisingly beautiful too. It was difficult to believe that the anguish of the last few hours had not etched itself in deep lines on the smooth skin. But . . . A sharp pain in her chest reminded her that the day was still not over, that shortly she would be expected to present herself downstairs where, under the carefully concealed scrutiny of the servants, the farce would have to be played out until the end.

A sob broke from her lips, and she began to pull at the buttons from her dress, feeling relief when she was free of its folds and could toss it carelessly on to the bed. Her original inclination to throw it into a corner seemed childish now and pointless; besides, it was too late. She looked at the broad gold band which had joined the sapphire on her finger. Much too late. She and Rudi were married now, and there was nothing she could do about it.

This morning when she had first dressed for her wedding there had been a welling excitement in her attitude, a kind of tremulous anticipation of the happiness that lay in wait despite the circumstances of their marriage.

No, she shook her head, the luminous eyes dark with pain as she made the silent denial, she had hugged to herself the realisation that she was about to marry the man she had loved all her life, that tonight, after the guests had gone, when they were alone together, perhaps all the misunderstandings would be swept away, perhaps if—no, *when* they made love, Rudi would find that with her it was

different, that after all she would be able to make
him forget Klara.

This morning she had had the self-confidence, the
conceit to believe it was possible. But that brief
glimpse of him in his bedroom cradling Klara against
his chest had dispelled any such illusion, had forced
her to see that the other woman possessed him with
something much more potent than mere sexual
attraction, something that Arabella could not begin
to understand.

Only a flicker of something like rebellion rose
inside her, a reminder that she was after all her
father's daughter, unwilling to give up even when
the circumstances seemed least auspicious. Abruptly
she rose and went to the bathroom, the notion that,
in spite of everything, she wanted Rudi von Schlegel
and was prepared to fight for him still only half-
formed. But by the time she had showered and was
rubbing soft perfumed creams into her body, it was
becoming more insistent.

When she went downstairs, her fingers sliding
with smooth confidence over the silky wood of the
banister, Arabella had the light of battle in her
eyes. And not just that, but a glow of barely
controlled excitement and anticipation. She hadn't
got quite as far as admitting how she expected the
evening to end, but that was merely because she
refused to allow such a mind-bending distraction to
confuse her intention.

As it was, the sigh, quickly suppressed but quite
discernible and identifiable as admiration from the
maid who passed her in the hall, gave her the boost
she needed. Not that such a fillip was really
required, for her mirror confirmed that she had
never looked better.

She had chosen to wear a distractingly lovely
dress in a fluid silky material, its softness clinging to
her body like a caress and its shade almost picking
up the flash of brilliance from her engagement ring.

Quite deliberately she had matched them, and hoped Rudi would notice the similarity and draw conclusions from it. Narrow straps left her shoulders bare, and the deep neckline of the tiny bodice gave more than a hint of firm curves.

Round her throat was a short silver chain—a simple thing, but it was her father's gift for her twenty-first birthday and so especially valued. It seemed appropriate that she remind herself that but for him she would not be in her present situation . . .

The clinging skirt of her dress flared about her legs as she made her way to the room where she knew Rudi would be waiting, and her heart thumped so loudly against her ribs that she felt its agitation must be apparent as she turned the handle. At once he turned to greet her, and in that instant the expression on his face caused all her sophisticated self-possession to desert her; she was transformed into the inarticulate, tongue-tied adoring teenager she had been when they first met. But then the light she had glimpsed, had most likely imagined, was switched off, and the mocking cynicism which was determined they keep up appearances for the sake of the servants returned to his eyes as he took her fingers to his lips.

He had shaved again. That knowledge, an absurd throb, was caused by the smoothness of his skin, by the faintly familiar scent of his cologne, and it made her rising agitation almost impossible to control. What man would go to such lengths to maintain a pose, unless . . . Her mind veered wildly.

And he had changed, of course. Gone the dark formality of the suit he had worn for the wedding; now he was dressed in plum-coloured trousers and white ruffled shirt open half-way to his waist and showing more dark skin than she could cope with. He was wildly, almost wickedly handsome, and his hair, which had been slicked down for the ceremony, was now thick and shiny and springy, simply inviting

her to thrust her fingers through and . . . She
swallowed. Just as—thinking like this was so
dangerous but irresistible—just as she longed to
slide her hands in the open front of his shirt, to
make contact with the warm breathing flesh and . . .

'You look utterly beautiful, Arabella.' Was there
a note of huskiness there, or was that too wishful
thinking? She tried to smile but failed, trembled
when he touched her upper arm, his fingers brushing
against the side of her breast, releasing a thousand
quivering emotions.

Hungrily she watched him go to a small side table
to pour drinks, saw the long sensitive fingers hover,
each action apparently designed to heighten her
awareness of him, to make her long to . . .

'To us.' Now he didn't even try to hide his
mockery as he raised the goblet slightly. 'And to
marriage.'

Arabella didn't reply, but took the glass to her
lips, closely watchful as she faced him over the rim,
wrenching away only when he threw himself into a
seat opposite. For a moment he lay back, his
attention concentrated on the golden liquid, eyes
drawn together in a morose frown.

'Caroline is an attractive girl.'

'What?' Irritation with herself for having been
caught gazing brought the heat to her skin, and
surely today *she* ought to be the only woman
admired. 'Oh, yes.' Now it was her turn to
study her glass, long dark lashes sweeping down
protectively. 'I think she is quite taken with
Gunther. That's why . . .' Abruptly she stopped.
With her own future so nebulous, this was not the
moment to hint at visits from her friend. Even
tomorrow seemed a fragile possibility. If Rudi made
any reply, she didn't hear, for just then a servant
appeared to let them know that dinner was served.

A small round table, dark, highly polished,
reflected the glow from three tall pink candles set

among scattered magnolia blossoms. As she took her seat, feeling Rudi's fingers brush against her bare shoulder, the scent from the flowers rose so overpoweringly that she almost wept. Such a romantic setting; the servants had gone to great lengths to make it so. Her finger reached out to touch a petal where a bead of moisture lay like crystal. And yet it was all for nothing.

Doubtless it was because her glass was so frequently refilled that she drank more than she was used to, and when the maid had at last gone she became aware that her head was spinning. But instead of realising why, she allowed reality to slip away from her; all the recent happenings receded and she was reliving the bliss of their early relationship, allowing herself to be beguiled by first love.

The coffee did little to bring her back to her senses. Certainly not enough, for when, with all the shyness of a traditional bride, she told her husband that she was going upstairs, she took no trouble to hide the tenderness of her feelings, the feverish expectation which threatened to overwhelm her.

She sat in her bedroom brushing her hair with languorous expectation, most of the earlier anguish of the day wiped from her mind. All that mattered was that today she had married the man she had always loved, that any moment now the door would open, he would come across the deep carpet towards her. Feverishly she watched the reflection of the door behind her, trying to control the hammering of her heart against the lace of her nightdress.

White, naturally. She wondered if later Rudi would understand how suitable that colour was, in spite of what he had made of her relationship with Kulu. Beautiful, too, of course. Tiny bodice, even lower than the dress she had worn at dinner and leaving so much less to the imagination as it caressed her tenderly rounded figure. The matching négligé swept back from the shoulders, spoiling nothing of the nightdress which was as dreamily elegant as a ballgown.

A tap at the door took her whirling round, heart beating still more wildly when it opened and Rudi came into the room. Contrastingly he was dressed in black, a silk dressing-gown belted about his waist with a red sash, black pyjama trousers, bare feet curled into the deep pile of the carpet.

For a moment he lay back against the glossy white of the door, a dark silhouette which drew attention to the ravaged starkness of his expression. For a moment Arabella felt all her recent excited conjectures slip a little. Wordlessly she got to her feet, stood facing him, saw his dark eyes absorb every detail of her appearance, lingering on the softly inviting swell of her breast then at last returning to her face.

Slowly he levered himself away from the door, walked silently across the room till they were close. So close she had to raise her head to look at him. So close he must have been blind to avoid the look of appeal in her eyes.

'Rudi . . .' On his name her voice trembled, she felt the sting of tears and blinked them away.

'Arabella . . .' His voice was deep, sardonic and something about it caused a frisson of nervousness in the pit of her stomach. He smiled then, and there was nothing reassuring about the flash of white teeth against tanned skin. And yet she had the idea he was holding himself tightly in control, afraid to relax. His hands she saw were thrust deep into the pockets of his robe and he made no attempt to reach out and touch her. And that, just that, was all she yearned for.

'You need not feel afraid, *mein Schätzchen*'. That word which had always caused a ripple of joy, a shiver of desire, could do so even when his every inflection robbed it of tenderness. 'But we must keep up the façade, *nicht wahr?*'

'Wh–what do you mean?'

He didn't reply but walked to the bed and threw himself on to it, his feet kicking away the carefully folded cover. 'Come,' he invited extending his arm across the other pillow, 'come to the marriage bed, Arabella.'

She began to shake her head, but in spite of herself her feet moved across and she lay down beside him, her head falling back on to the pillow, her hair spreading across in a drift of dark silk. Apprehensively she turned her eyes towards him, almost offering her lips but finding none of the reassurance she sought.

But then quite dispassionately he leaned over her, smiling when her hand went to her throat, then bending his head so their lips touched. She had half expected his mouth to be hard and punishing, showing none of the persuasiveness she remembered and longed for. But she was wrong, he was gentle, his lips tempting hers to part as beguiling as the hand that came out to cover her breast, then more bewitching still to brush aside the lace so that soft flesh was tormented by delicate teasing fingers.

Arabella felt a shudder run through her, admitting that any last restraints were melting under the magic of his lovemaking. Her hands were reaching out towards him, yearning to feel the crisp silkiness of his hair beneath her fingers, but then he broke away; he was looking down at her with bitterness, although she was then too shaken to make that interpretation.

'Rudi.' She watched him swing himself from the bed, her voice faltering from shock, unwilling to accept what her brain was telling her.

'That,' his grin was wolfish, 'should satisfy the servants, don't you think?'

'Wh–what do you mean?' Pride made her rise,

pull the edges of her négligé about her and turn to
face him.

'I should have thought it was clear enough, my
dear . . .' He walked to the door and stood, one
dark eyebrow raking upwards towards the tumble
of hair on his forehead. 'Earlier you made your
feelings more than clear. All I ask is that you
preserve outward appearances until we can effect
some remedy of the situation.'

'But . . .' her anger came out like a sob, forcing
her to bite her lip ferociously, '. . . you said you
wanted . . .' The word stuck in her throat, refusing
to be spoken.

'I said I wanted what?' He advanced again and
stood glaring at her.

'You said you wanted a wife and . . .'

'Oh, that. I confess that's what I thought I wanted
at the time. A wife and children. In that order.'
Sudden fury and contempt were blazing in his eyes,
she had to clench her hands tightly to stop them
rising instinctively to ward off an expected blow.
'Do you *understand* me?'

'No.' She was utterly bewildered. 'You said you
wanted children and that I . . .'

'I have no intention of forcing on any children I
might have a mother who can't stand the sight of
me. *Now* do you understand?'

She stared, her mind totally blank and wholly
bewildered by the scene. Vaguely she shook her
head, her lips formed the word no, but she knew
she had not spoken.

'Today,' his air of menace was intended to
intimidate, but she refused him the satisfaction of
flinching, 'you showed me how utterly you hold me
in contempt. Presumably it suits your way of life to
remain with a man who has no intention of marrying
you . . .

'What do you mean?' Drained of all emotion, she
could make no sense of what he was saying.

'I mean your employer. I suppose these last few days you've been nursing resentment at being forced from his arms into mine.'

'I choose whose arms I go to.'

'Really?' He gave the impression of enjoying himself. 'You mean you go to the highest bidder.'

'No one forced you to bid.' Her sole defence was to throw back every caustic word he spoke, to try to hide the lacerations caused by his bitter accusations.

'That is quite true, and you can't despise me more than I do myself. I was a fool to believe you were still what you had once been, despite all the evidence to the contrary.'

'But you already . . . knew that when you suggested we marry.'

'As I say, I was a fool.' Showing he had had enough, he turned away, going to the door and putting his hand on the knob; Arabella could see the knuckles gleaming white. 'But if you expect me to accept the insult you were preparing for me earlier today, then . . . well, even I am not such a complete fool as that.' He shrugged as if it hardly mattered. 'I would not have believed it possible for the girl you once were to become the woman I'm looking at now.' The door opened and closed. And Arabella stood staring at the white paint, unable to believe or understand what was happening to her.

CHAPTER NINE

SURPRISINGLY there were no tears as Arabella lay, still and suffering through what was an endless night. She simply lay, in solitary comfort and misery, gazing blankly into the darkness, wondering what twist of malevolent fate had brought Rudi along to this room just before the marriage ceremony. It was against all the teasingly referred-to traditions which had insisted they must not meet before setting out for the Town Hall in Rosenheim. Even though, as she now remembered, Rudi had refused to be bound by any promise, although like his mother and Lise she had thought he was being deliberately provocative, trying to add to the general excitement by whipping up a little hysteria. She too had laughed, not imagining for a moment that he meant what he said.

'Arabella and I are not having an ordinary marriage'—his eyes had rested with special meaning on his bride's blushing face as he made his statement—'so normal rules don't apply.'

Ach, no,' his mother agreed delightedly. 'When was any marriage ever ordinary? And when did you, Rudi, ever behave in an ordinary fashion? That would be too much to ask. But still, do not take any risk, my son; you know how unlucky it would be to see Arabella before you set off for the ceremony.'

'As I said, Mutti, things with us are different from all others. Remember, a week ago you did not know of her existence.'

'No?' Frau von Schlegel raised an eyebrow. 'You think not?' It was a puzzling reply, suggesting the opposite of what had been stated, one which Arabella couldn't begin to understand. But she had little time to think about it, for Rudi changed the subject with the quiet determination he could exercise when it suited him.

But if only he had taken notice of the old tradition. If he hadn't found her wearing that dreadful dress—now she knew she would never have had the nerve to go downstairs wearing it—he would not have chased away any good fortune that might have been waiting for them. At the last moment she would have changed back into her beautiful wedding dress, would have presented herself in the best possible light to the guests and . . . Yes, and to Rudi as well. No matter how much she would have hated her father and Frau von Schlegel to be spectators of such spoiled petty spitefulness, she could have borne even less for Rudi to learn of that black, vindictive side of her nature.

But the man she loved—at last she allowed the humiliating admission into her thoughts—the man she had always loved must now have formed the lowest possible opinion of her. So low—she tortured herself with the cruel facts—that he could not bear to spend a night in her company.

At last, but not till dawn was streaking the sky, Arabella fell into an exhausted sleep.

When she woke and glanced at the clock she gave a gasp of astonishment and threw back the covers. Eleven o'clock; whatever would the servants think? Then, as she remembered what they very likely would think, she felt the colour flow into her cheeks.

At least—when she had dressed she surveyed herself in the mirror—at least this morning she meant to have it out with Rudi. She would tell him exactly what had caused her behaviour yesterday, try to convince him that the mourning dress had been simply a reaction, foolish and over-dramatic, she was prepared to admit, but a reaction nevertheless to seeing the love-scene between him and Klara.

Besides—she fiddled with the broad leather belt securing the calf-length skirt and silk blouse striped in tan and navy, tucked a navy kerchief into the neck—she must learn to live with the fact that her husband had a mistress, maybe even more than one, if she knew the truth. Her eyes were shadowy with pain as she tried to face the facts. She would offer her explanation to Rudi, tell him of the shattering experience of seeing Klara in his arms and leave him to judge. He was a reasonable man and would surely understand . . .

Nevertheless, her stomach was churning nervously as she walked downstairs and across the hall to where breakfast was served. She opened the door and went inside, drawing a deep breath when she realised that Rudi was there. Somehow she had imagined he would be up and away before this, and she was not prepared to see him so soon.

Politely he rose, leaving the sheaf of papers he had been studying spread out over the polished surface. Bending his head, he kissed her cheek, a formal gesture, with lips so cold and distant she was at once chilled. 'Arabella.' A shade of concern in his voice, perhaps, but she must not allow herself to be misled. 'You slept well?'

'Not really.' It had not been her intention to sound so pert and childish. 'You would hardly expect it.' She took the seat he had pulled out for her. 'And you?'

The cynical smile made a brief appearance at the disturbing mouth. 'As you say, one would not expect it. The coffee has just been made, but if there is anything else you would like, then . . .' He indicated the bowls of fruit and rolls, plates of yellow butter, thick golden honey.

'Coffee is fine.' She reached out for the pot, placed as usual on the hot tray. 'I don't want anything to eat.'

'Maybe you should. Remember my mother thinks you are too thin.' He rustled his papers, giving the impression she was interrupting his work, so she didn't trouble to reply. Besides, she was afraid that she might burst into tears if she even tried.

'I thought,' she was on her third cup of coffee before she was able to speak, 'you would have breakfasted ages ago.'

'No.' With apparent reluctance he put down his papers and looked at her. 'I had a long ride first. Oh, remember when you want to ride there is a suitable horse. We can find you something better if . . .'

'If I stay—is that what you meant to say?' The words broke indiscreetly from her lips.

'No, that isn't what I was going to say. You see,' he rose from his seat opposite and came round to where she was sitting, forcing her to bend her head back so he could be in no doubt about her mutinous expression, 'I have been thinking, Arabella.' His hand came out towards her, fingers circled her neck, caressing the tender skin so that every nerve end was frayed and ragged. 'We must not act hastily, do things in a temper and then have regrets for the rest of our lives.'

'I . . . I . . .'—conscious of little but a fingerstroking thoughtfully at the nape of her neck, she could hardly think—'I don't know what you mean.'

'No?' He crooked an amused eyebrow, which removed some of the tension from his face, yet revealed how tired he looked. 'I think you do. But in the meantime'—quite abruptly he deserted her, walked to the other side of the table and collected his papers—'I have had an unexpected crisis with my publishers, and they want some revisions completed. As always,' he was frowning over what were clearly publishers' proofs, 'they want things done at once. But perhaps in this case it's as well; it gives us time . . .' His sudden smile was charming, made her heart turn over, and she almost expected him to click his heels and announce, 'I am Schlegel'. 'I don't suppose you can type.'

Again she was transported back through time, by the very same question, and as before she was inclined to lie, to say that of course a hundred words a minute were nothing. But discretion won the day and she shook her head, depriving herself of an excuse to be closeted in his study, door closed, utterly alone with him . . . Oh—she gave herself a mental shake and almost smiled, for after all, how could it possibly improve their relationship if she messed up all his work?

'Pity. Then maybe you'll excuse me. I must just get on with some work. Besides, we could both do with some time . . . to think. If you like I'll have the car brought round; perhaps you'd like to drive into town and do some shopping.'

That suggestion was barely worth considering, and Arabella shook her head. And if she had been less absorbed by the grains at the bottom of her cup she could hardly have missed seeing how his eyes followed the dancing movement of the hair about her face, his expression one of puzzled depression.

His sigh was quickly controlled as she raised her head, and all she noticed was total absorption in his work as he walked to the door, that and the easy elegance that had always been so much a part of him. Even this morning, dressed casually in a pair of hip-hugging trousers and checked shirt, sleeves folded back to show powerful forearms, there was something arresting about him. She started, swift colour staining her face, when she realised that he was waiting for an answer.

'I said,' luckily he appeared not to notice her reaction, 'are you sure you'll be all right until lunch?'

'Perfectly.' She resisted the temptation to say she had little choice. 'In fact I think I'll take up your suggestion and go for a ride.'

'If you can wait, we could go together. I'll be through by lunch; maybe we could have a picnic . . .'

'No, don't trouble.' Deliberately she gave the impression of long-suffering. Far be it from me, her air of cool detachment implied, to interfere with anything so absorbing as your work. I'm just the girl you married yesterday, but I understand my place in your life. 'I shall enjoy it.' Lacking the courage, she omitted the word alone, allowing her manner to say it instead. It gave her a tiny bit of satisfaction to see his mouth tighten in irritation.

'Well, see you wear a riding hat. There are quite a few and you should find one to fit.'

She didn't answer, but when he had gone she poured out the last of the coffee, cupping her hands round the warm bowl and trying to blink the tears away. What does it matter to you? she asked. If I crack my skull or break my neck then you would be none the worse. Who would miss me, after all? She caught her lip, biting it fiercely to control her despair.

Oh, hell! Her expletive was meant for herself. Why hadn't she told him? Why hadn't she done what she fully intended when she left the bedroom? If she had explained just what had caused her to act as she had done, then by now things between them could be, if not mended, then maybe patched up so that they could begin to heal themselves.

Abruptly she rose from the table, and a moment later was running upstairs to change into jeans and a pullover. A ride in the fresh air would help to clear her mind. For the past week she had hardly had time to know if she was on her head or her heels. Decisions made at nights were abandoned in the morning, and she seemed unable to plot one firm course and stick with it. She would go for a ride and try to see things in their true perspective.

And the countryside was looking particularly lovely with all the tints of autumn beginning to colour the trees and hedgerows. As she trotted along a path she felt some of the pain and worry ease away from her. She ought not to have been so abrasive when Rudi had suggested a picnic; it would have been fun, and, who knows, a carefully packed bottle of wine, a blanket to lie on down in that little hollow beside the stream . . . she paused on a small hillock looking towards a patch of soft grass bounded on one side by rippling water. Miraculous changes had been affected by much less.

Feeling more optimistic, she pulled on the mare's head, pressed the heels of her heavy brown shoes against the fat sides to encourage a little more speed, a hint which the brute placidly ignored as she headed for home. The ride had been a help; for one thing she was ravenously hungry, interested in food for the first time in days.

She was singing lightly under her breath as she entered the hall and took the stairs two at a time. A quick glance at her watch reassured her that she had enough time, and when she reached her bedroom she had a leisurely look in her wardrobe before deciding what she should wear.

The bedside telephone gave an aggressive little ring and without thinking she lifted the receiver and stood listening. It took just a second to understand that she was intruding, that whatever had caused the machine to jangle was wholly accidental, and she didn't even try to follow the spate of rapid German. Not, that was, until some liquid inflection about the female voice told her exactly who was speaking. Then, quite slowly, the telephone which had been half-way back to the cradle was raised again to her ear.

The painful weight had returned to her chest, was throbbing away with all the intensity she had ever known, but it was only when she heard her husband's voice that she tossed the thing away from her in savage distaste, heard it bang once or twice against the furniture as she threw herself on to the bed.

'Rudi, *mein Lieb* . . .' She heard the raised voice querying the unexpected noise, then distantly Rudi's reassurance. And what he had to say was so liberally interspersed with endearments that Arabella thrust her hands over her ears to stifle the sound.

It was only when she had been lying on the bed for a few minutes that she realised the conversation was over and, wiping away the angry tears with the back of her hand, she reached for the receiver and replaced it. Aferwards she was grateful that she had acted so sensibly, for a moment later there was a knock at her door and Rudi stepped into the room before she could answer.

Arabella didn't trouble to hide her tear-stained face; let him make what he liked of it, and if he imagined she was weeping for her own situation then that was all right. Really, she no longer cared. She merely pushed herself into a half-sitting position and looked without speaking.

'Arabella.' If he noticed her woebegone expression then it clearly did not matter to him, his recent conversation undoubtedly occupying all his thoughts. 'I'm sorry, I shan't be with you for lunch after all.' Anger rose threatening to choke her but she gave no sign. 'I have to go out unexpectedly, *mein Schätzchen*.' How *dared* he use that endearment to her?

'That's all right.' Perhaps he would deduce that she meant something much more positive such as, 'I'm delighted.'

'You're sure.' Unexpectedly he sat on the edge of her bed, took her hand in his. 'Sure you don't mind?'

'Why should I mind?' She managed a tiny shrug.

'No reason.' His shrug was equally casual, but she had the satisfaction of seeing his lips tighten as he rose and stood looking down at her. 'But as I said, I'm sorry, and I'll try to make it up to you this evening. Tell me,' he spoke as if he were humouring a child, 'which would you prefer, going somewhere we can eat and then dance? Or if you would rather, they're having a musical evening at the palace at Herrenchiemsee and . . .'

'Opera again—I find it so boring.' Although she wanted to hurt him it was painful to watch the shutters come down over his eyes.

'I didn't say it was opera, but if you would prefer to go dancing, then . . .' He seemed to be angry rather than wounded.

'Let's leave it, shall we?' Deliberately she interrupted, swinging her feet on to the floor and walking away towards the window. 'After all, you've no idea when you'll be back.'

'I'll be back in time for that, I assure you.'

'Don't hurry on my account.' And a moment later the sound of the door closing told her he had gone.

She ate a small lunch, her appetite having faded again, and she could sense the disapproval when Berthe, the jolly girl who came daily from the village, removed the scarcely touched food. Afterwards, Arabella drifted aimlessly about the garden before dragging one of the reclining chairs into a sheltered position behind a hedge of high beech and lying down, meaning to read a fashion magazine she had brought from Berlin.

It was inevitable, after the previous night's insomnia, that she should drift off to sleep. In any case, she excused herself drowsily as she gave in to

the overwhelming pleasure of that state half-way
between sleep and wakefulness, it was the only
thing that offered some relief from the misery she
had been enduring for as long as she could recall.
Perhaps, if she concentrated sufficiently, she might,
might dream of Rudi as he used to be. And of
Arabella, some demon of justice demanded the
admission, as she had been.

She had no idea how long she slept, but she woke
with a start to realise that the sun had gone down.
She felt quite chilly and shivered, imagining the
sound of a voice ringing in her ears. Reaching for
her cardigan, she struggled to her feet, for the
moment confused and barely able to understand
where she was.

'Frau von Schlegel!' Good heavens . . . The
realisation came as a shock—they must be looking
for her.

'*Ja, hier*, Berthe.' She emerged on to the
lengthening shadows of the lawn, watching in some
amusement as the stout figure of the maid came
hurrying towards her, puffing and panting. Then, at
the expression on her face, a twist of apprehension,
fear clutched at the pit of her stomach. Oh, no.
Her heart began to pound, a chill of sweat broke
out on her forehead. No. No!

'Frau von Schlegel! *Gott sei Dank*! *Ihr Vater* . . .
Your father . . .' Berthe managed a few words of
English, then relapsed into her own tongue, but
slowly in spite of her agitation.

'Keep calm, Berthe.' Arabella barely noticed the
ease with which she was dropping into the language;
she was mentally reeling from the shock of what
Berthe had told her, was trying to absorb all the
details which had been received just a few minutes
ago by telephone.

'Yes, I understand, Berthe. My father's very ill
and in intensive care.' In view of his medical history
there was little doubt what that meant. Fear

increased its grip, and she castigated herself for not realising the probability of such an occurrence. It took her just a second to make up her mind. 'Ask Heinrich to bring round the car at once to take me to the airport.' She glanced at her watch. 'I'll go upstairs and pack a bag and . . .'

'But Herr von Schlegel will be back soon; you must wait for him.'

'No, Berthe, I cannot.' Now she was running up the long curving staircase. 'I must get to my father or . . . it might be too late.'

And it was sheer chance that got her to the airport just half an hour before a flight left for London, but she didn't feel safe until the plane was skimming along the runway; only then did she feel safe from pursuit. And now, blindly she looked at trees and bushes flashing past, then roofs as they lifted off, now she wished she had been less precipitate in what she had scrawled in the letter she had left for Rudi. Initially the note had been for the benefit of the staff, left prominently on his desk, the name inscribed on the envelope for anyone to see. But inside, the message had been conveyed in the most cursory terms, until the last line, that was, when all her pain and unhappiness spilled out. 'So you see,' tears had splashed on to the words, 'it has all been for nothing. *Nothing*.' And she hadn't even done him the courtesy of signing her name.

She came back to life when the stewardess, wheeling the trolley down the aisle, offered a drink which was refused, then, discovering that she was still clutching her ticket, she made to push it into the outer pocket of her travel bag. Her fingers encountered something firm, and it wasn't until she pulled out the hardback book that she remembered what she had done with her elusive copy. In all the rush and turmoil of leaving her Berlin hotel, of being enveloped in the preparations for the hurried wedding, she had forgotten where she had put it. Not that she had had a great deal of free time to read, but she had been anxious to find out if it told her anything about her husband. She had even searched in the library in the Schloss, but although there were several copies of the book, the English version had not yet joined them. French, Dutch, Italian, Spanish, as well as the original German, but she was fluent in none of these. It would have been easy to ask Rudi if he had a copy in English, but so averse was she to her reactions being noted that she had shied away from that. His image looked at her from the back cover, and she passed a finger over the beloved features.

'It's good, you know.' She turned to see her neighbour, a middle-aged businessman, nod towards what she was holding. 'I couldn't put it down till I reached the last page. My wife complained about the light being on half the night.'

'Oh?'

'Have you started it yet?'

'No. I'm just going to . . .'

'Then I'd better shut up.' He grinned. 'I'd hate to spoil it for you.' He looked at Rudi's picture which lay uppermost. 'They actually say most of it's true. What a man!' He shook his head admiringly.

Yes. One finger caressed the unsmiling photographic image. What a man. Arabella could still remember, with a shudder, her feelings when Berthe had come towards her over the grass and she had imagined something had happened to Rudi. And the sense of relief—how terrible to have to admit such a thing—the relief, the total overwhelming sense of *release* she had experienced when she had understood that Rudi was not the cause of the anxiety etched on Berthe's face. What kind of daughter am I? she asked numbly. Then she sighed, opened the book and began to read.

When they reached Heathrow, Arabella walked

through the 'Nothing to Declare' checkpoint in a total dream, her mind unable to absorb the significance of the message. Or at least, unable to believe it. If she did allow some credibility to seep into her understanding of the story, her whole world would be topsy-turvy; two and two would no longer make four.

'Taxi!' Emerging into the hurly-burly of the street, she raised a hand automatically, hardly aware of her incredible good fortune in finding transport so immediately, but sinking on to the cool shiny leather of the seat. 'Westminster Hospital.' But her mind, instead of being preoccupied with the possibility of finding her father already dead, was still busy with the implications of Rudi's story. In fact, she found it impossible to resist pulling the book out again, re-reading a passage which seemed of special significance. And when she had satisfied herself she gave a shaky sigh, her mouth trembled, and the lovely eyes looking out at the teeming traffic of the capital were filmy with tears.

'But Miss Smythe . . .'

'Frau von Schlegel,' Arabella interrupted without thinking, then at once felt her cheeks burn.

'What?' The senior staff nurse looked at her in surprise. 'I thought you were Mr Smythe's daughter.'

'Yes. My married name is von Schlegel.' Married and yet unmarried, she told herself bleakly. And all because of my own stupid fault.

'Oh, I see.' The staff nurse spoke huffily. 'Well, here it says next-of-kin Miss Arabella Smythe. I've just come on duty, and . . .'

'*I've* just flown in from Germany in response to a telephone call that my father was seriously ill.'

'Seriously ill. Well,' the nurse sniffed and looked disapprovingly at Arabella's snugly fitting jeans in champagne leather, the matching waistcoat worn over a wool blouse in various shades of green, 'I suppose some people think a broken leg is a serious complaint, but it's common enough, and only in the rarest cases considered a threat to the patient's life.'

'A broken leg?' Abruptly Arabella subsided on to a chair in front of the Sister's desk, this evening in the charge of her senior staff nurse. 'I thought . . . But I was told he was in intensive care . . .'

'Maybe just for a few minutes while some checks were being done. I see . . .'

'I thought it was his heart. You see he . . .'

'As I was going to explain.' Staff Nurse Hodge's look was repressive. 'I see Mr Smythe has a history of cardiac arrest, so possibly it was purely precautionary, but now your father is in the main ward. You can go in now. There's still quarter of an hour of visiting time,' she added regretfully.

'Thank you.' Sensing that she was on the verge of dismissal, Arabella got up and walked to the door.

'Fourth bed on the right.' Staff Nurse Hodge replaced the file on patient Smythe and turned her attention to the pile of notes she had been studying before Arabella arrived.

'Daddy.' It was just a whisper as she slid her fingers into his, uncertain if he was awake, not wishing to disturb him if he was asleep. But the eyes opened at once, tried for a few uncomprehending seconds to focus before his face cleared and he smiled, tried to push himself into a sitting position, grimaced and uttered a protesting cry when he encountered the resistance of the pulley suspending his leg above the bed.

'Arabella!' Reproach struggled with delight in his voice as he sank back on to the pillows. 'Oh, it's good to see you, love.' He squeezed her hand as she bent to kiss him, then they both laughed as she wiped her tears from his cheek.'

'No wonder you're crying!' His own eyes were suspiciously bright. 'Being dragged away from your honeymoon just because I tripped over Miss Cavendish's cat and fell down the front step.'

'Is that what you did?' She sniffed, ripped a tissue from the box on his locker, blew her nose fiercely. 'I can't leave you for ten minutes, can I, or you get into trouble.'

'That's about it. If it's not one thing,' the bright eyes clouded briefly, 'it's another. Tell me, is Rudi with you?'

'No,' she was absorbed in riffling through her bag, having no idea what she was looking for, 'Rudi's been caught up with some problems over his latest book; he had gone to his publishers when the message came. Only,' smiling with what she hoped would pass for satisfaction, she produced a Biro and a notebook, 'I didn't stop to think, just shot off for the airport. When I get back to the flat, I'll ring and let him know what has happened.' The lie came easily enough. 'He'll be worried when he knows. Now,' she waited with her pen poised above the paper, 'tell me what you need. I'll hang on at the flat till you're on the mend, and can collect anything. I don't suppose,' she looked reproving, 'you bothered to pack a bag before you went out looking for Miss Cavendish's moggy.'

'No, I didn't think.' He grinned. 'I *could* do with one or two pairs of pyjamas, and a dressing-gown and slippers for when they let me up, although . . .' he banged his knuckles on the plaster which enclosed his leg from knee to ankle, ' . . . I doubt if I'll be out of bed for a bit. But Arabella, love,' some thought had occurred to him, 'I'm not having you staying here, not when you and Rudi were planning to be off to Kashmir.'

'Kashmir?'

'Oh, don't say . . . Oh, Bella . . .' He looked so totally crestfallen she could have smiled. 'I thought . . . I mean I never thought . . . Oh, blast it, have I spoiled the surprise for you? I thought

Rudi would have told you by this time! Now, not a word. When he pops his surprise you're to behave as if you've never *heard* of Kashmir. Only he told me he had something a bit special planned as a honeymoon trip. Part of the way on that royal train—you know, the one built for some Maharajah in the days of the Raj. Then off to stay in a Sultan's palace in Kashmir. Oh, I could kick myself for letting the cat out of the bag!'

'Miss Cavendish's cat, I presume. Anyway, I wouldn't even try if I were you. At least not till your broken leg is better.' As the bell rang signalling the end of visiting time, Arabella got to her feet.

'Thanks, darling. For coming, I mean.' For a second he held her, brushing her cheek with his lips. 'And thank Rudi for letting you come and oh . . . for everything. You know what I mean.'

'I know.' This time she had to force a smile, and as she walked the length of the ward she was thinking, not of her father who ought to have been her immediate concern, but of the book which she was half-way through and which she knew she must sit down and finish the moment she got back to the flat.

As she read the final word she put her fingers to her cheeks to wipe away the tears. They had been flowing off and on since, foddered with a huge pot of tea and some biscuits, she had slumped exhaustedly into a chair in front of the gas fire as soon as she got in from the hospital. She gave a deep, shuddering sigh and put the book on the arm of her chair, the picture of her husband uppermost so she could enjoy the pretence that he was looking at her. Oh . . . her fingers traced the outline of his features, you idiot, you darling . . . idiot. Why, why didn't you tell me?'

For she had no doubt whatsoever that she, heavily disguised as Lori Brown, was none other than the enchanting heroine of *An Old Affair*. Notwithstanding that Lori was American, notwithstanding her blondeness nor her position as a translator for the American Forces in Berlin, notwithstanding every kind of red herring, too much of what happened between Lori and Ludo, the hero of the book, a character which apparently he had never denied was Rudi von Schlegel, too much of it had been experienced by them when they had first met that idyllic summer in Berlin.

One scene in particular, which in the later unhappiness she had tried to obliterate from her mind, was related in tender, sensuous detail, such detail that reading it she had relived the actual pain, weeping as she had done at the time, when Ludo or Rudi had drawn back from the inevitable culmination of the passion that had blazed between them.

She could remember as if it had been yesterday. Arabella sat hunched in one corner of the sofa, watching the gas flames flicker and splutter but seeing that scene as if she had never expunged it from her mind. They had been swimming in the Havel, the same water that lapped at the immaculate lawns of his house in the Grünewald. There had been eight or nine of them in the party, but gradually they had separated into twos and threes until only two of them pulled themselves out of the water on to the tiny island, soft and green and utterly private, even the distant shouts of other bathers hardly penetrating such a secret hiding place.

They found a small patch where the sun beat down through a circle of trees on to turf as soft as velvet, a positive invitation to lie down together. And for a long time it was enough for them to be there thigh to thigh, touching, their lips in almost constant contact, the slip of cool skin on skin an unbearable delight.

And then with a groan, Rudi abandoned what she had despairingly imagined was total control; she was forced back on to the grass, his lips were more savage, more demanding, as impatient as her own, and his fingers were pulling at the strings which held the two pieces of her bikini in position. Not that she made any move to stop him, in fact she kicked them aside, rejoicing in the roughness of his chest hair against her breast, rejoicing in the certainty that at last, at last, her mind could hardly cope with the explosion of joy, her cravings would be totally fulfilled.

But then, when her heart seemed about to burst from her breast, she heard him make a muttered, anguished imprecation and roll away from her. For a moment Arabella lay gasping, then, opening her eyes, she stared at the irregular patch of blue sky lit by the dazzling noonday sun. She knew herself to be in shock, and had no control of the silent tears which flowed down her cheeks. Moving her head stiffly, she could see the outline of Rudi's figure; he had an arm extended to support himself against a tree trunk, the dark head was bowed towards his chest, his gasping breath was being brought slowly under control. Even as she watched he bent down, retrieved his swimming trunks with hers, and when he had drawn his on over the powerful thighs he turned with a faint grin, holding hers out towards her.

'Arabella.' There was warmth in his tone, a warmly tender amusement. 'Forgive me.'

'Forgive you?' Unable to bear it, she rolled over on her side, determined he would not see her tears. 'What is there to forgive?' She bound her arms across her breast. 'Just that at the last minute you found it wasn't what you wanted after all.'

'You know that isn't true.' His fingers touched her shoulder, then moved quickly. 'It's what I want more than anything. What we both want, I hope, but . . .' There was a pause when she was so busy dealing with her own feelings of frustration and inadequacy that she had no curiosity to spare for him. 'Look, put on your clothes, Arabella.' It didn't seem funny to either of them to describe two tiny pieces of cotton thus. 'Otherwise I can't think.'

'Well, please turn away.' New to a situation like this, she couldn't deal with it easily.

'But of course.' And she sensed him standing there, eyes turned away as she struggled with the clammy swimming costume.

'Let's go, then, shall we?'

'Of course.' Determined to be blasé, she had no idea how much of her feelings, her hurt she was revealing.

'But,' his raised hand, not quite touching, made her pause, 'don't imagine it was easy for me to stop, Arabella.' The dark grey eyes seemed black, their expression causing a shudder to rack her. 'I should have remembered how dangerous it would be to come here with you, like this.' A sweep of his hand made her understand he was speaking of their semi-nakedness. 'Unprepared.' He watched the colour race into her face as the implication of his words percolated into her senses. She dropped her head, looking down at his legs, dark, sprinkled with hair still darker, she was remembering how strong and forceful they had felt against her own, and . . .

'I could not forgive myself if you became pregnant.' The concern in his voice brought her attention back to his face.

'But . . .' She was about to say that as they were to be married anyway that hardly mattered, but the remoteness of his expression stopped her words.

'I know what you're thinking,' it seemed she had no need to explain, 'but one isn't always in control, and if anything happened to me . . .'

'Don't be silly, Rudi.' Something in his manner was making her nervous. 'Nothing is going to happen to you. Nothing.' She raised her hands and beat against his chest as if her determination would protect him. 'Nothing, do you hear?'

'Of course you are right.' But there was a wariness about him almost immediately dispersed as he patted his chest in a familiar gesture, smiled lopsidedly. 'I don't suppose you happen to have a cigarette with you. I would do anything for a smoke right now. I need something to calm my nerves which you,' he gathered her close to him with a pretence at menace, 'have ripped to pieces this afternoon.' But almost at once, before the fiery emotions between them could be fanned into consuming life, he moved away, touching only her fingertips as they began to force a way through the bushy undergrowth to re-enter the water.

Each detail was etched on her memory, had apparently been remembered by him as well. It was described in such loving tenderness that the anguish assailed her as if it had happened just yesterday. Even then, apparently, the shadow of a possible separation was clouding their relationship. Later, he had cursed himself for not taking the girl into his confidence, but their affair was so carefree, so tender, so perfect that he had wished nothing to shadow it. Besides, she was so young.

Shortly afterwards, when he had been forced by his father's imprisonment to make his clandestine visit to the eastern zone, when he had been picked up by the authorities and placed on a prolonged period of surveillance and house arrest, he had lots of time to regret that decision. But gradually, as the time passed and he was held as a guarantor for his father's good behaviour, he had adjusted to the realisation that she was lost to him for ever, that she was doubtless married, there would be children and that for her it was probably better so.

At last Arabella got up from her seat in front of the fire and began to remove her clothes. What she

wanted more than anything was a warm shower and
a good night's sleep. Tomorrow would be time
enough to think what to do next. Still, she couldn't
help wondering if everyone had been as moved by
the reflectiveness of the novel as it reached the final
page, when the hero, freed only by the death of his
father, was finally allowed to leave East Germany
with his mother. He was still in love with the
American girl, admitted he would always love her,
and yet the desire to seek her out, to discover what
had become of her, such an obsession in the years
immediately after their separation, had dwindled
and died. Now, he admitted in the penultimate
chapter, he was too afraid of doing her some harm,
of disturbing whatever happiness she had found for
herself by an intrusion into her present life. And
besides, his experiences had, he knew, wrought
drastic changes in his personality; the same could
have been equally true of her, and he refused to
risk shattering the perfection of the memory.

No, he would never seek her out, he told his
readers, but each time he went into a room with
strangers he was subconsciously searching, looking
for a woman just a bit taller than average, hair of
warm glossy silk, a girl who would immediately feel
his eyes on her. Some day, the book ended,
somewhere I know that I shall see her. But I fear
the changes will have been too great. For both of
us.

All the time Arabella was in the shower she
tormented herself with images of what might have
been. If she had been less jealous, less abrasive,
less determined to show him how little he meant to
her now—if she had been any of those things, then
their marriage might have had a chance. But she
was not the girl he had fallen in love with. And by
this time he must be very much aware of that fact.

Sighing, she stepped out of the stream of hot
water on to the fluffy mat, tied a towel about her

sarong-style and padded through to the bedroom, rubbing briskly at her hairline where the water had penetrated her cap.

Then, just as she was about to reach for her nightdress, the doorbell of the flat rang with a peculiarly aggressive impatience. Stunned, she looked at herself in the glass, rather surprised that the agitated beating of her heart didn't show. Who on earth could it be at this time of night? A glance at the clock told her it was after midnight, and crazily that subdued her anxiety, for what more likely than that Caroline, having heard of the accident and assuming that Arabella had flown home, was calling in on her way back from some excursion or other? It wasn't entirely unexpected, for she had a habit of begging a bed at the last minute when she had done something mad like missing the last train home.

Arabella adjusted the bathtowel more firmly under her arms and went to the door, reaching it just before the bell rang for the second time.

'I'm coming . . .' She turned the handle and threw the door back. 'Caroline . . .' But the words faded from her lips as she saw her husband standing there. She took a step backwards, and he advanced into the hall, closing the door firmly behind him.

For an eternity they stood there looking at each other, she trying to conceal her agitation, trying to persuade herself that the expression in his eyes was not the tenderness she longed for. After all, how could she expect him to go on loving her after the way she behaved? It was as he had suspected, the changes were too great; where once she had been a sweet, trusting, *loving* eighteen, now she was suspicious, shrewish and . . . She shivered.

'Arabella.' Reaching out, Rudi touched her shoulder.

'Don't . . .' She couldn't bear it, to have his

touch wakening all those feelings which might never be assuaged.

'You are cold.' He appeared not to notice her intervention, or, having noticed, had decided to disregard it, for both hands were now on her skin. One circled her neck, pulled her close to him, and his mouth was on hers in a bewildering kiss which set fire to her senses.

'Rudi.' Even as she breathed his name her arms were reaching up, fingers were twisting in his hair, and it didn't matter when the towel loosened and dropped to her feet.

Instantly she was swept up, he was shouldering his way through the open door of the bedroom, placing her gently on to the soft, quilted cover. For a long moment he knelt on the floor, eyes blazing down. Then he spoke. 'I forgot to tell you'—his voice was husky, even shook a little—'that I love you. Never for an instant in all the years have I stopped loving you, wanting you, And I shall go on loving you till the day I die.'

All the tensions which had for so long been knotted inside her eased, dissolved in the fire that was thrusting its way through her body. She watched him toss his jacket on to a chair, pull at his tie, and as he came towards her, lithe and sinuous, she rose to meet him, arms outstretched in welcome.

'Rudi'—making the confession her voice broke; she knew that if she waited the moment would be gone—'I . . .' She gasped at the sheer sensual pleasure as his powerful arms cradled her close to him. ' . . . I love you too. Never, never anyone else.' His hands were about her waist, mouth on her cheek, she heard a groan deep in his chest.

'And all this time, I've been afraid . . . afraid that you and Kulu . . .'

'Not Kulu,' Arabella allowed herself the pleasure of fingertips moving delicately over the warm silkiness of his skin. 'Not anyone; I have . . .'

'Not now, *mein Schätzchen*. Later.' Fingers tracing the length of her spine inclined her more intimately towards him. 'Now we begin to sweep away all the torments of the past.' Delicate kisses feathered down her throat, blood fevered in her veins, a pleasured moan broke from her lips . . .

When she stirred in the dawn her familiar bedroom at first seemed strange, she knew she ought to be in her room at the Schloss. But then the night's wild indulgences came back to her mind, and she smiled faintly and turned, arms reaching out instinctively for the dark shape by her side.

'*Liebling*.' His response was immediate and they took slow delight, touching, gently laughing, whispering, coaxing till they were swept together on to a pinnacle of total rapture from which the descent was slow and blissful.

'*Liebchen* . . .' Much later Rudi's voice was soft with sleep. 'Forgive me; last night I quite forgot to speak of your father. But I did know that he wasn't as seriously ill as you thought. I rang the hospital from the airport and they said he had broken a leg.'

'I don't know why I didn't do that.' It was convenient for her to forget that yesterday she had been running from an impossible situation as much as coming to see a gravely ill father. 'Obviously Berthe got the message slightly wrong.'

'I only just missed you, you know. If I had been ten minutes earlier I would have caught your flight.'

But then I would hardly have had the chance to read your book, she thought, but before she could speak he went on.

'Why, Arabella, did you pretend that you and Kulu were having an affair? You can have no idea how . . . inhibiting wild jealousy can be.'

'I think you assumed we were and I just encouraged you to believe it. Now, I can't think why I did. I suppose it was because I didn't understand, then, why you had had to leave me, I mean. And then . . . I was wildly jealous of Klara Steyr.'

'Of Klara?' Rudi's tone was contemplative. 'I suppose you could have been. But utterly without reason, you know.'

'But . . .' She no longer had the inclination to throw back at him everything she knew, but still, it was best that her doubts should be out in the open. 'The day we were married . . . I came along to go to Caroline's room and saw you with her.'

'You saw me with Klara! I'm sorry you did, Arabella. And I suppose that was why you decided to get back at me by wearing the black dress.'

'That was awful of me.' Humiliation made her voice low so he had to bend his head close to hear. 'I would never have gone ahead with it, you know. It was just a momentary impulse, but I think too much of your mother and my father to do that. I was just so angry that on our wedding day . . .'

'And when I came along to your room,' he spoke wryly, 'determined at last to tell you what I had been aching to confess since that first night at Frau Steffan's, I found you in deepest black. What could I think but that you were still in mourning for Kulu? I was so angry and jealous I could have killed you!'

'But now,' she whispered provocatively, 'you're rather glad you didn't.'

'Rather glad,' he smiled as he smoothed the tumbled hair from her forehead, 'and I hope you know too that your jealousy for Klara was equally pointless, although . . .' he considered, 'I won't deny completely that it was a misunderstanding I was half inclined to encourage . . .' He caught a hand raised playfully to strike. 'You know, there was never even the hint of an affair between us.' He paused. 'You have read the book?'

'Yes.' She was puzzled. 'On the plane and before you arrived, but . . .'

'So soon?' He laughed. 'Well, that's enough to put any bestselling writer in his place.'

'Oh, I bought a copy, but . . . well, I suppose I was suffering from emotional exhaustion and could hardly keep my eyes open at night, and besides, I mislaid my copy and only found it on the plane.'

'Excuses, excuses. But anyway, you remember Dieter, who . . .'

'Yes.' Difficult to imagine that one of the book's minor tragic figures could have anything to do with what they were discussing.

'Who was in love with Gretl and determined to get over the Wall . . .'

'Yes, but . . .'

'Klara is Gretl.'

'Oh, poor Klara!' She recalled how the young artist escapee had died in the arms of the woman he loved, remembered weeping over her hysterical suicide attempt. Then another shattering idea swept away all thoughts of Dieter and Gretl. 'Rudi, how did you get out? You didn't . . .'

'No, I didn't come over the Wall. For one thing I had my mother and Lise with me. Let's put it like this; the authorities didn't want to keep me for ever. And just about that time I was able to get the manuscript smuggled out to the West and it began to attract attention. I applied for exit visas for all three of us, and after the usual bureaucratic time-lag they were granted. I don't know what their reasoning was, whether they thought it would be best to avoid publicity; they probably realised I was unlikely to have accepted a refusal lightly. Or maybe they were just relieved that I was fairly even-handed in my criticisms of the various political régimes I touched on. But most likely of all, it's just that things are easing very gradually. Even there attitudes are changing slightly, although nothing would persuade my mother or Lise to risk going back even to West Berlin. Their experiences

have taught them to be very suspicious. But anyway,
we were talking about Klara . . . You'll find it hard
to believe, perhaps, that she suffers terrible bouts
of depression; she's had all kinds of psychiatric
treatment, has dabbled in drugs, and from time to
time I get an SOS and have to try to help.
Remember, Dieter is the friend of my youth. That
and nothing else would have kept us close over the
years, but now, she realises at last that things have
changed. Yesterday I cleared that up finally. Now I
think she understands.'

For just a second Arabella felt a pang of sympathy
for Klara, something she would hardly have believed
possible before. But it was so easy to believe that
Klara had imagined that his affection for his
boyhood friend would be translated into something
much more positive. *That*, she was fairly certain,
was the kind of therapy Klara Steyr expected in the
end from Rudi von Schlegel.

'Anyway,' Rudi gathered her more comfortably
into the crook of his arm, 'let's forget about Klara
and Kulu for the time being. There are so many
questions I haven't got round to asking, but they'll
all come out eventually. The only regret I have
right now is that instead of taking advantage of
your father's position to force you to marry me, I
should have seized the opportunity to make you fall
in love with me again.'

'Again?' she smiled dreamily. 'I couldn't fall in
love with you *again* when I had never stopped.'

' . . . And I'm wondering if it's too late to begin.
Do you think if I did this,' he slid a persuasive
hand across her skin, stifled her gasp with his
mouth, 'or this,' he laughed, a deep throbbing noise
deep in his throat, 'you would decide to come away
with me?'

'Away?' There was a provocative question in the
way she flicked an upward glance at him, while her
mind, for no reason she could understand, filled

with images of Eastern houseboats on glassy lakes with distant snowy peaks reflected on gleaming water.

'Tell me, where would you like us to go for a honeymoon?'

'Honeymoon?' Her fingers tangled with his. 'I thought that was what we were having now.'

'This is merely a delightful interlude. Tell me where you would like to go.'

'With you, I want to go anywhere. But tell me what you have in mind.' And she lay with her cheek against his pounding heart, her fingers tracing the firm outline of his chest, moving provocatively over the warm silken skin as he began to tell her. But . . . he didn't get round to finishing the story until much later.

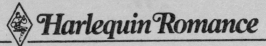 **Harlequin Romance**

Coming Next Month

2869   CARPENTARIA MOON   Kerry Allyne
Photographer Eden arrives to be tourist director at an Australian
cattle station, asked by Alick, a friend, but finds the station is
owned by his older brother who regards her as the latest girlfriend
Alick is trying to dump!

2870   WINNER TAKE ALL   Kate Denton
When a campaign manager recommends that her boss, a Louisiana
congressman, find a wife to dispel his playboy reputation, she
never thinks she'll be the one tying the knot!

2871   FORCE FIELD   Jane Donnelly
For a young amateur actress, playing Rosalind in an open-air
production in Cornwall is enjoyable. But being emotionally torn
between the estate owner's two sons, a sculptor and an artist, is
distressing—until real love, as usual, settles the matter.

2872   THE EAGLE AND THE SUN   Dana James
Jewelry designer Cass Elliott expects to enjoy a working holiday
until her boss's son unexpectedly accompanies her and their arrival
in Mexico proves untimely. She's excited by the instant rapport
between herself and their Mexican host, then she learns that Miguel
is already engaged....

2873   SHADOW FALL   Rowan Kirby
Brought together by a young girl needing strong emotional
support, a London schoolteacher and the pupil's widowed father
fall in love. Then she learns of her resemblance to his deceased wife
and can't help wondering if she's just a substitute.

2874   OFF WITH THE OLD LOVE   Betty Neels
All of Rachel's troubles about being engaged to a TV producer
who doesn't understand her nursing job and expects her to drop
everything for his fashionable social life are confided to the
comfortable Dutch surgeon, Radmer. Then, surprisingly, she finds
Radmer is the man she loves!

Available in November wherever paperback books are sold, or
through Harlequin Reader Service.

In the U.S.
901 Fuhrmann Blvd.
P.O. Box 1397
Buffalo, N.Y. 14240-1397

In Canada
P.O. Box 603
Fort Erie, Ontario
L2A 5X3

Can you keep a secret?

You can keep this one plus 4 free novels

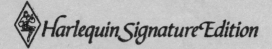

Penny Jordan

Stronger Than Yearning

He was the man of her dreams!

The same dark hair, the same mocking eyes; it was as if the
Regency rake of the portrait, the seducer of Jenna's dream, had
come to life. Jenna, believing the last of the Deverils dead, was
determined to buy the great old Yorkshire Hall—to claim it for
her daughter, Lucy, and put to rest some of the painful memories of Lucy's birth. She had no way of knowing that a direct des-
cendant of the black sheep Deveril even existed—or that James
Allingham and his own powerful yearnings would disrupt her
plan entirely.

Penny Jordan's first Harlequin Signature Edition *Love's Choices* was an
outstanding success. Penny Jordan has written more than 40 best-sell-
ing titles—more than 4 million copies sold.

Now, be sure to buy her latest bestseller, *Stronger Than Yearning*. Available wherever paperbacks are sold—in October.

Harlequin Intrigue
Adopts a New Cover Story!

We are proud to present to you the new Harlequin Intrigue cover design.

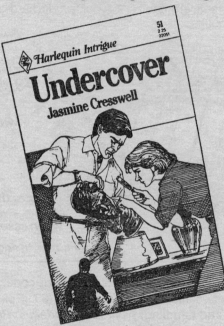

Look for these exciting new stories, which mix a contemporary, sophisticated romance with the surprising twists and turns of a puzzler . . . romance with "something more."

Plus . . . we are also offering you the chance to enter the Intrigue Mystery Weekend Sweepstakes in the October Intrigue titles. Win one of four mysterious and romantic weekends.

Buy the October Harlequin Intrigues!

ATTRACTIVE, SPACE SAVING BOOK RACK

Display your most prized novels on this handsome and sturdy book rack. The hand-rubbed walnut finish will blend into your library decor with quiet elegance, providing a practical organizer for your favorite hard-or soft-covered books.

Only $9.95

Approximately 16" x 8" when assembled

Assembles in seconds!

To order, rush your name, address and zip code, along with a check or money order for $10.70* ($9.95 plus 75¢ postage and handling) payable to *Harlequin Reader Service*:

Harlequin Reader Service
Book Rack Offer
901 Fuhrmann Blvd.
P.O. Box 1396
Buffalo, NY 14269-1396

Offer not available in Canada.

BKR-1A

*New York and Iowa residents add appropriate sales tax.